THE FELLOWSHIP
OF THE FLAME

Chosen Generation
Mission 1 : Eden
Brad Parker
Copyright © 2015 Brad Parker

Published by Seraph Creative in 2015
United States / United Kingdom / South Africa / Australia
www.seraphcreative.org

Typesetting, Design & Layout by Feline
www.felinegraphics.com

ISBN 978-0-9923554-9-4

Dedications

To my wife and three children, I dedicate this book in love. You bring me joy, daily. You bring me light and give me the reason to get up and try to be the husband and dad I know you deserve.

I also dedicate this book series to a chosen generation. My heart is that you grow into everything God intended for you in the fullness of His loving plan and desire. You are a Joshua generation, becoming a perfect bride, acquiring His promises as Sons of God.

In the early stages of writing this book, I thought you needed more Bible knowledge. By God's grace, I have come to Paul's revelation which he shared with believers in a town called Ephesus. I see now that you need to grow in the faith and knowledge of the Son of God, becoming mature to the point that you attain the whole measure of the fullness of Christ. I pray this book series opens a portal into the depths of God. I hope you are soon revealed as the Sons of God.

CONTENTS

CHOSEN
GENERATION

Mission 1 : Eden

Prologue

If you happened upon the documents in this book then you were chosen to read it. This is no coincidence.

My name is Theta.

I am the angel who wrote this account to be sent to the General of the Lord's Army, Michael the Archangel.

Here you will find my letters to the Archangel, and a written account of how it all started. You may be wondering to what it is that I am referring. I am speaking about the beginning of the Joshua Generation.

I was assigned to five teenagers who will go down in history, because at this time most Christians believed the world was only going to get worse, but then the truth was revealed to a company of burning hearts.

By reading these documents you are agreeing to help me. Warning! Once you decide to read these documents, you become part of the story.

Do not read any further if you are not ready to go on this journey and if you are not prepared to take on this mission. This is an adventure that started before the world began. You are living in the most exciting time, but with excitement and joy comes sacrifice and danger.

If you are ready to face the dangers, both within and without, then let us continue. If not, then please put this down and never so much as touch it again.

If you are ready, then let us begin at the beginning. It all started several years ago. I think it was in 2002.

Dear Michael Archangel to our Lord,

Theta here. As you instructed, I am writing detailed notes about what is happening with those you intrusted to me. I decided to start from the very beginning, as you suggested. Please send my regards to the counsel and the fellowship.
For His Glory,
Theta

    This all started one strange night when I was summoned to leave my post. I was told to come quickly to meet with the Lord's highest-ranked angels at the most top secret meeting place on the third moon from the planet Zoe. The place was called Mt. Rhema and the meeting place was a hidden crystal cathedral.

    I tripled light speed, trying my best to arrive promptly. With great anticipation I flew, my hair and robe flapping wildly as I went. Maneuvering as trained, I landed with ease on Mt. Rhema, gray dust whipping around my feet. As I approached the cathedral with excitement and curiosity I wondered why I was being asked to meet at the sacred cathedral. Who was I to be called to such an awesome place? I was a class-two angel with a small assignment of watching an inner-city playground for the last twenty years in Chicago, Illinois.

For many years I had dreamed of working somewhere more exciting—not that I didn't enjoy the Chicago mission, but I often grew bored and hoped one day I would receive an adventurous mission.

With each step my curiosity amplified. Finally I reached the steps leading up to the cathedral doors. Looking up at the castle-like structure, I was speechless. It was shining like a diamond against the black, starlit sky.

I opened the large, glass door, and as I walked down the long corridor, I noticed tiny angels the size of fireflies lighting the path through the hallway into the inner chamber and down to the altar. The path to the altar was decorated with holograms. Artistic works of art, colorful pictures of prophets, apostles and archangels stretched across the upper limit of the corridor and hovered above me. The golden passageway floor cast a warm, yellow reflection up onto my robe.

Instantly I recognized a sweet aroma of incense burning as I approached the inner chamber. I could see smoke rising in white, slithery waves from a small bowl set in the middle of the altar. There I could see the burning of incense at the altar of worship.

Looking around, I realized that the angels I was to meet

had not yet arrived. The only sound I heard was the soft, dull hum of tiny angels' wings buzzing. So I decided to take the moment alone to worship. I knelt at the altar and spoke words of praise, whispering softly, "To Him who sits on the throne and unto the Lamb of God and the Holy Spirit: Holy, holy, holy is your name for evermore."

Suddenly I heard a voice calling, "Rise, Theta."

Looking up, I was astounded. Before me I saw twenty of the highest-ranked angels in heaven. In the center, standing some twenty feet tall, in a robe made of pure, spun gold, was the Archangel Michael. His hands rested lightly on the hilt of his sheathed sword.

Taking a deep breath, I saluted, stating loud and clear, "Greetings, Michael, Archangel to our Lord. How may I be of service to our King?"

Michael smiled. I could tell he sensed I was nervous. "Greetings, Theta, and may the blessing of the great I Am, the Messiah, Savior, Lord and King be upon you."

From his robe, Michael pulled a sealed parchment. "This is to be read only by you, Theta, but before you read it, I have some good news. You have been appointed to the Fellowship of the Flame."

I could not believe my ears. The Fellowship of the Flame was a group of angels who were assigned to help the gospel pass from generation to generation.

"I do not know what to say, General."

"I take it you are honored, no doubt," said Michael. "You

have done well, watching your post for the last two decades. A workman is worthy of his reward. So, take this and read."

I reached up and took hold of the parchment.

Fellowship of the Flame
TOP SECRET:
- ☐ Mission Agenda: Pass Gospel to the next generation
- ☐ Action Plan: Train and disciple five teen-agers; The goal is for them to grow into everything God intended for them in the fullness of His loving plan and desire.
- ☐ Special Note: This marks the beginning of the Joshua generation, those who are becoming a perfect bride, acquiring His promises as they are being revealed to all creation as Sons of God.
- ☐ Location: Arkadelphia, Arkansas
- ☐ Trainees:
  - ☐ Randall Wisdom, Jr.
  - ☐ Katie Summers
  - ☐ Jude Tripp
  - ☐ Jill Denver
  - ☐ Gray Floyd

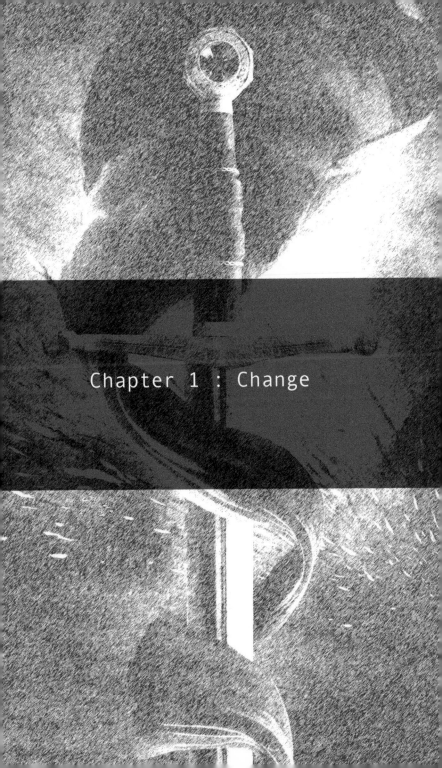

Chapter 1 : Change

Chapter 1 : Change

The story began with Ran Wisdom, the son of a missionary. It started on August 19, 2002.

Ran Wisdom gripped his carry-on bag tightly as the jet touched down on the Little Rock Airport runway. He hated landings, but even worse he hated the dreadful feeling he got when he thought about seeing his grandfather, Dr. Randall Wisdom, a Professor of Physics at a small Arkadelphia, Arkansas, university called Henderson State.

Ran dreaded spending two hours trapped in a car on the way to Arkadelphia with his grandpa to whom he secretly referred as "the professor." The professor was an intimidating genius and was now going to be Ran's new guardian.

The long flight left Ran's legs aching and his stomach empty. He brushed his bangs out of his face and nervously peered out the small window of the airplane.

He followed the passengers unloading and fought to get his luggage off the conveyor belt. Just when he was pulling off his bag, he thought he saw his grandfather. His stomach jumped, but thankfully he realized it was just some other bald man.

Seeing no sign of the professor, he walked outside and leaned his tall, strong body against the wall. His black, curly bangs fell into his eyes. Hunger pangs pulled at his stomach, so he made his way over to a nearby bench and rummaged through his bag until he found some airline pretzels. In total exhaustion he stared into space. He leaned back down in his bag for his drink and stumbled across a photo.

The photo was of his father, James Wisdom. Ran looked at his father's silly grin and whispered, "I wish you were here."

A teen-age girl about Ran's age, with red hair and

freckles, sat down beside him. She was wearing a blue tank top that read, "PRINCESS." Ran couldn't help but chuckle. He turned the other way, took a bite of his pretzel and looked at his photograph.

"Hi. I'm Jill Denver." She stuck out her hand. Ran turned around and shook it.

"Can you believe they don't serve peanuts anymore on airplanes? Where are you from?" Jill asked.

Before Ran could answer, she had another question. "Who's that in the picture with you—your dad? Where is he and why isn't he with you?"

It felt like she had asked ten questions before Ran finally got in a word edgewise. "Yes, that's my dad."

"Well, where is he?" Jill smiled and wrinkled her cute, freckled nose.

Ran did not want to talk about his dad. He didn't really want to talk to anyone. He looked at Jill. She sat beside him like he was an old friend, and Ran thought she looked like one of those strangers who would pester him with a hundred questions, even though she had just met him. He took his time to answer. "First of all, my name is Ran."

"Ran?" Jill interrupted, "I'm not trying to be rude, but that is a weird name."

"My name is actually Randall. I was named after my grandpa." Ran smiled, thinking about when his mother had given him his nickname.

"Okay, so tell me about your picture," Jill smiled, "and why you are traveling alone."

Ran was cornered. He didn't want to talk about the picture, his dad, or why he was traveling alone. "Hey, why are you traveling alone?" he asked.

"No! Not fair. I asked first. Your turn, Ran, the man." She poked him.

"Ouch. Okay. This is a picture of my dad, and I'm traveling alone because he could not make it," he said, hoping she would leave it at that.

"No! Not enough. I have to sit here and wait for my ride, and I've already read two books today. I want to know all about you. So, why couldn't your dad come with you? I want to know everything."

Ran's stomach turned. He did not want to talk to this stranger anymore. He wished Jill Denver would catch the next plane out. He could see she was not going to leave him alone, so he took a deep breath.

"Well?" Jill said, tapping her bright, red, painted finger-nails on the concrete beside him. "I'm not going anywhere until you tell me."

"Okay, already. First of all, my dad is . . . I mean was, a missionary in Jakarta, Indonesia," Ran said apprehensively.

"What do you mean 'was?' Did he retire?"

"No . . ." he sighed, "he was martyred."

Jill crinkled her nose again, but not in a smile. "Martyred? What does that mean?"

"Martyrs are preachers who are murdered just for being Christians and trying to share their beliefs with others."

"Oh . . ." Jill looked down. "I'm sorry . . . I didn't know. I shouldn't have bothered you."

Ran knew this would be the response, but he did not want to embarrass the poor girl. "Look, it's okay. I know you didn't know."

She was quiet and he felt awkward. Finally, she looked up, "Can I ask you one more question? I mean . . . unless it offends you."

"No, I guess that would be okay," Ran said.

"Where were you when it happened?"

Ran closed his eyes and recollected, "I was supposed to

meet my dad, but I was busy with a friend. I was teaching him about football, and in return he was teaching me martial arts."

"You play football . . . I'm sorry . . . go ahead." Jill smiled.

"Well, like I was saying, I was supposed to go pick up my home school textbooks and go meet him, but I went out with my buddy to practice football." Ran tried to stall. He didn't want to think about the next part.

He closed his eyes again in recollection. "Anyway, when I got to the church, it was completely burned down. There were only ashes and smoke. The officers told me that three men locked him in the building and then set it on fire."

"That's awful." Jill paused for a moment. She looked up, "Did the police find out who did it?"

"Yes. They were three Muslim fundamentalists."

"What's a fundamentalist?" Jill asked.

"That's a Muslim who kills Christians and believes they are doing it for their god."

Jill looked angry. "That doesn't make any sense at all."

"I agree," Ran said.

Then they sat in silence for a while. It was the first silence Ran had had since he met Jill Denver. It was nice but it did not last long.

"Did y'all have a funeral yet?"

"The missionary people had a small memorial service. There was no burial because . . . well there was no body found," Ran said.

"Ran, why are you in Little Rock?"

"My grandparents live in Arkadelphia, Arkansas. Besides, that is where I grew up. I guess I would still be living in Arkadelphia, but my mom got sick two years ago, and that's when my dad quit pastoring and went into missions." Ran regretted mentioning his mom.

"Your mom was sick? Did she die, too?" Jill's expressions showed that she was a girl of compassion.

Fortunately for Ran, he did not have to give details about his mother's death, because just then Jill's parents called for her.

"I've got to go. It looks like my parents finally got here."

"Hey," Ran stood up, "you never said why you were traveling alone."

"Oh, I went to visit my real dad." She pointed to the car at the curb, "That's my stepdad."

Ran waved to the man with a mustache sitting behind the steering wheel of his Mercedes.

Jill stuck out her hand, "Well, it's been nice meeting you and listening to the history of your life. One more question?"

Ran rolled his eyes.

"Are you going to home school or public school?"

"I'm going to public school," he replied.

She gave her most adorable smile, "I guess I'll see you at school, then."

"You mean you live in Arkadelphia, too?"

The car horn honked again, and the bald man gave her a stern look.

"Yep! Small world, Ran, the man." She waved, then jumped in the backseat. Ran watched the car zoom away.

Ran put the picture of his dad back into the bag and said to himself, "Well, Lord, I guess that's one friend I've made. You sure know how to pick them." He laughed.

Sitting on the bench, eating pretzels for another hour, he thought about his dad. Then, all of a sudden, he was jerked to attention by the sound of a stern, recognizable voice.

"Don't spoil your dinner on cheap pretzels, Randall, Junior."

It was the professor. He was a tall, lanky man with outrageously long eyebrows, long white goatee, a shiny, slick, bald head and a thick German accent.

"Yes, sir, Grandpa," stammered Ran as he got to his feet.

His grandfather hovered some two feet over him. Looking down his nose, the professor said, "Are those your bags?"

Ran nodded his head yes.

"Well, don't just stand there—load them in the trunk." The professor went to the driver's side of his white 1978 Cadillac Seville, slithering into his seat like a wraith of oily smoke.

Gray clouds formed quickly across the open Arkansas sky, and thunder began to roll. The professor pointed the car southwest into the light rain on Interstate 30. On the ride home Ran did not want to talk to the professor, so he placed his headphones over his ears.

"What's your problem, boy?" the professor scrutinized, jerking the headphones away. "Didn't your father teach you manners? Now, it will take us about two hours to get home, and I want your full attention as I lay down the rules."

"Yes, sir." Ran gulped.

The professor talked over the sound of windshield wipers squeaking back and forth. "I don't know how your father was running things over there in Indonesia, but if you're going to live with me, we are going to have some discipline. That means no more home schooling . . . do you understand?"

Frightened, Ran nodded his head.

"All right! Rule number one: Studies come first. I know from talking to Grandmother that you have some wild dreams of playing professional football or being a musician." The professor smirked, "That is a bunch of poppycock. The chances of your making it in either profession are against you. So education comes before activities.

"Rule two: No television . . . at all! We don't own one and you won't, either.

"Rule three: Stay out of my study. I'm working on writing a book, and if my files get damaged or deleted, then I have to start back over again.

"Understand so far?"

Ran's face was flushed. He was sweating. What was wrong with this guy?

"Well, do you or don't you?" The professor could stare through a steel door.

"Yes, sir, I understand," Ran stammered.

"Good! Rule number four: If you're going to go to church, you'll have to go with your grandmother. But note, I don't like it one bit. However, I promised her I wouldn't stop you."

The professor paused for a moment, and Ran took a look into his flat, black eyes. He couldn't see an ounce of kindness.

Then the professor said deliberately, "I don't see why you'd want to serve some god like that after what happened to your father."

That was all Ran could stand. He didn't mind being bossed around, but he was not going to let the professor talk about his father or his God.

"Wait one second, sir. My father, who happened to be your son, went over there to help those people. And you can't blame God for what they did to him in return."

The professor pulled the car to the side of Interstate 30 and stopped the car. The rain was pouring down in buckets, and the sky was dark. The professor's face was lit up by a flash of lightning. "Excuse me?" he seethed, his fist upraised.

"Nothing, sir . . . I was just—," Ran said, recoiling to his side of the car.

The professor fumed, slamming his fist into the steering wheel, then gripping the wheel tightly so that his knuckles turned white. "Rule number five: Never question your grandfather!" Feverishly he slammed the car back into gear and sped back onto the interstate, spewing gravel onto the road behind them.

Arkadelphia is a small town that is the home of two universities, which are literally across the road from each other on none other than University Street. One is a private Baptist university, and the other is a public university.

Professors own homes in residential areas that are a comfortable distance away from their students. The homes are mostly European in structure.

Ran's grandparents' house was a nice, raised, cottage dwelling built by a Methodist minister in the early 1860s. The style was reminiscent of New England saltboxes and incorporated a full cellar, which contained the kitchen and dining area.

The Cadillac pulled into the driveway of the Wisdoms' home at around 5:00 p.m.

Ran was relieved that he was going to get away from the professor and got excited when he saw his grandmother standing behind the screen door. Her name was Jane Wisdom, and she was a short, stout, German woman, who

seemed to fear nothing and could outpace a quarter horse.
Ran called her Granny Wisdom and had fond memories
of her reading C.S. Lewis' book The Lion, the Witch, and
the Wardrobe to him when he was nine years old. She
was a devout Christian and the reason Ran's father, James,
became a minister against the professor's wishes. She had
tried for years to win over her husband, but he would not
yield.

When she saw them arrive, she ran out to meet them
with a brown umbrella in hand.

The professor only allowed Ran a few minutes to visit his
grandmother.

"Is dinner ready?" he asked.

"Yes, dear, it's on the table."

"Good. Let's wash up."

When dinner was over, the professor stood and
commanded, "Come along, follow me. I will show you
to your room." He marched ahead. "You're going to be
staying up in the attic."

Granny Wisdom followed. "Grandpa, honey, are you
sure we should put Ran in the attic? It is so dark and
damp."

"Of course, I'm sure." He kept marching until he got
to the end of the hall. Reaching up he pulled a long string.
A door in the ceiling creaked open, and a long ladder
descended. "This is how you get to your room."

Ran looked at his grandmother.

"Oh, please, let him stay in your study," Grandmother
pleaded in Ran's defense.

The professor looked down at Ran. They both were recalling the rules he had set forth. "Absolutely not! The study is off limits."

"The boy will catch a cold in the winter and burn up in the summer in there," Granny pleaded.

"He's a tough boy, Jane. When I was young we didn't have heat or air, and I turned out alright."

Granny Wisdom turned around and walked back down the hallway. "You sure did," she mumbled.

"Jane? What did you say?" The professor was livid. Looking down at Ran he whispered, "Boy, all I want is to keep peace around this house. It's important that I keep your grandmother happy, or she'll start in on me and I won't be able to get anything done." He paused. "Look at me. . . Don't think I'm going soft. I'll let you stay in the study . . . wait! Don't get excited yet. You've got to promise me that you won't touch anything in there.

"Do you understand?"

Ran nodded his head.

Granny Wisdom hummed an old gospel tune as she turned the office couch into Ran's bed. She was wearing a fluffy, old, pink housecoat. It was the same one Ran had bought her at Christmas two years ago.

She smiled at him. "Don't be scared of that old coot, Ran." Her eyes were sparkling blue, just like his dad's. "You are going to do just fine, living here." She reached out her soft, wrinkled hand and touched his face. "Don't you worry about anything." She turned and walked out of the study, humming her tune.

Chapter 1 : Change

Ran crawled into bed. Everything smelled like old people. He didn't mind. It felt sort of like home. His stomach felt sick; perhaps it was the ride home with the professor, or maybe because he had eaten something other than rice and fish, or perhaps it was because he was alone. At age fourteen, he was an orphan.

If he could just go back to the day his father was murdered, maybe everything would be different.

He remembered their last conversation, when his dad told him to pick up his new home school textbooks and meet him at the church. But Ran did not listen to his dad that day. Instead, he went and picked up the books and then stopped off at his friend's house to practice football. No one knew this little fact . . . except Jill Denver. Besides a complete stranger knowing, it was his guilty secret, and it was the reason he could not sleep at night. Ran secretly felt he was the reason his dad was murdered. If he'd just met his dad at the right time, they could have left the church and the attack never would have happened.

Quietly to himself, Ran whispered, "Why, God? Why? I was so stupid. If I had known what was going to happen, I never would have been late. Why didn't Dad come with me to get my books? Why did I have to lose both Mom and Dad? And why do I have to live with this maniac?" He couldn't think of the words that described the bitterness, the unfairness of it all. "Sometimes I wonder if you are really out there, God."

Tears soaked his pillow. All of his old friends probably would not remember him. Ran knew how hard it was to fit into public school. There were so many cliques. He remembered that there was one friend who had written to him a few times over the last two years—Gray Floyd. "Maybe, just maybe, Gray will help me fit back in." With the one hope to cling to, Ran fell asleep for the first time in several nights.

A few hours after Ran was asleep, Granny Wisdom quietly entered the professor's study and sat on the edge of the bed to pray for him.

"Dear God, I know this is a hard time for Randall, Jr. He is too young to suffer so much. God, I know you know our pain. Help little Randall, Lord. And God, help me as I raise him. Help me to raise him the way I raised his father, James. I am getting old, Lord . . ." she looked down at her wrinkled hands . . ."so I know this is going to be hard, but you have always given me the strength. As you said in your word, 'I can do all things through Christ which strengtheneth me.' Amen."

Tears ran down the wrinkles of Granny Wisdom's pink cheeks and onto her pink robe. She kissed her grandson on the forehead without waking him. Finally she retired to bed.

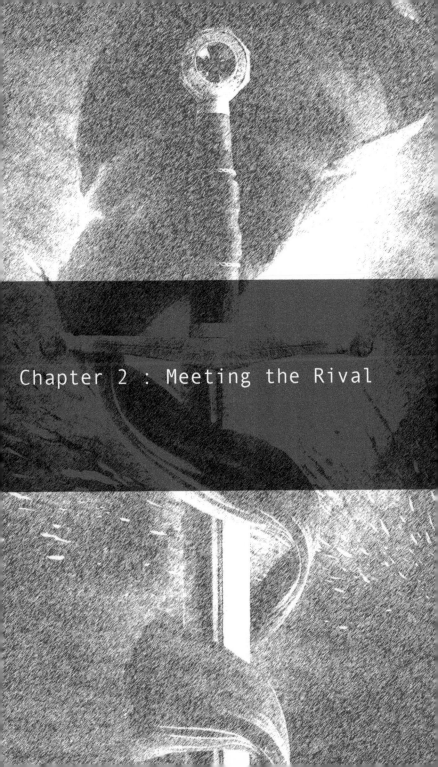

Chapter 2 : Meeting the Rival

Meeting the Rival

Granny Wisdom woke Ran early Saturday morning to take him shopping for school. He barely had time to read the newspaper at breakfast before she was calling for him to get in the car. Reading the newspaper was odd for a fourteen-year-old, to most, but Ran's dad, James, insisted he read every section. James would even quiz Ran on current events.

The car ride was short and pleasant. When they arrived at the strip mall, it was full of busy shoppers, searching through back-to-school sales. At a clothing outlet, Ran uncomfortably tried on clothes in the dressing room as Granny Wisdom waited for him outside the door, insisting she see him in each outfit.

"That's a nice color on you, but I hate those pants. They are too baggy. Don't go off to school looking like some hoodlum." She pulled up his pants from the back, making him feel like a two-year-old. He started to argue, but resisted the temptation. Who could argue with Granny Wisdom?

"Grandma, I already told you that you don't have to buy me new clothes. I have clothes to wear," Ran said.

"I do what I want.

"Well, did you see that, Ran? My goodness, the way the girls look at you. In my day we would have never," she smiled.

"See what?"

"You are as clueless as your grandfather. Those girls have been over there, giggling and looking at you, for ten minutes."

"They're not looking at me that way. They're probably just laughing at these baggy jeans. I'd better go change."

Granny Wisdom gasped. She was about to tell him how

handsome he was when she saw one of the girls coming toward them. Instead, she quietly made her way across the store to give Ran some privacy.

Walking towards Ran was a tall, blonde girl, who looked about his age. She was two inches taller than Ran, which made him stand up straight when she came near. She smiled at him. He was not sure why she was approaching him. Did she want to talk? Did she work at the store? His throat went dry, and he felt like bees were buzzing around inside his stomach.

She stepped forward. "Hi."

Ran gulped and managed to squeak a high-pitched noise that was supposed to be a hello. He felt his cheeks fill with heat and assumed his entire face must be red. He tried to regain his composure and manage a proper greeting.

"I mean, 'Hi'."

She smiled and didn't seem to notice his nervousness. "You're Ran Wisdom, huh?"

Ran wondered how she knew. After all, he had been in Arkadelphia for only a day. "Yes. I'm Ran."

"I'm Katie—you know, Katie Summers from the sixth grade. We had Mrs. Glover for our teacher."

Ran stared at her, trying to remember. The only Katie he remembered was this pudgy, short girl with braces who giggled all the time. And to Ran's surprise he could see a trace of that girl in her eyes. "Oh, my gosh! Katie Summers? I can't believe you remembered me."

"Well, you are a little taller and your hair is grown out longer. Remember, you used to have that buzz cut?" Katie took her hand and made a motion to show how short his hair was.

In the sixth grade, Ran had gotten a glob of Hubba Bubba bubblegum stuck in his hair and had an emergency haircut. He laughed out loud when he thought about it now. Ran shared the story with Katie, and they talked for several minutes about school and about Indonesia. He didn't mention his father.

Ran started to ask about his old friend Gray Floyd when two guys he didn't know interrupted the conversation. One of them had hair that was so blond it was almost white. He looked like he lived in the gym, because his neck was like a tree trunk. The other guy, who also looked like a muscle-bound mammoth, was shorter and his head was shaved completely bald. The one with the shaved head approached and talked in a voice that sounded like a bullfrog. "What's up, Katie? Coming to my birthday party tonight?"

"Hey, Jude, I was just talking to Ran Wisdom. We were in sixth grade together." Katie pointed at the two boys and said, "Ran, this is Jude and Vance. They're on the football team."

Ran waved. Then Katie said, "Hey, Ran was just saying that he wants to join the football team again. He's been living in Indonesia the last two years and didn't get to play. Maybe you guys can fill him in on what he needs to do to join."

Jude grunted out a laugh, "Tryouts were last month, dude. And besides, coach won't take someone who hasn't played in two years. Better luck next time." Jude's buddy, Vance, gave a cough that sounded like he was covering up a laugh.

Jude walked over and gave Katie a quick hug and said, "I got to jet. See you at the party—right, Katie? Anyway, hope so." He looked at Ran and smiled, "Tough break about football. I heard they are still holding tryouts for ballet." Jude and Vance walked off, giving each other a high five.

Ran felt awkward after they left. Just then Granny

Wisdom approached, smiling. "Ran, I see you made a new friend."

"Yes. Katie, this is Granny Wisdom—I mean my grandmother, Jane Wisdom. Grandma, this is Katie Summers. We were in sixth grade together."

Katie shared stories about Ran with Granny Wisdom, who chuckled loudly, embarrassing Ran. Finally Ran said goodbye, and he and Granny Wisdom left the mall.

On the way home he thought about Katie. She was undeniably pretty and nice. He thought she was probably nice because they knew each other in the sixth grade. Ran was not interested in girls yet. He was interested in football and getting into a good college.

He thought about meeting Jude and Vance. They were rude, and, worst of all, he did not feel like it was his last run-in with them. Football seemed out of the question now, but he was still going to talk to the coach on Monday. He looked out the window at the open Arkansas sky. A storm was on the horizon.

Chapter 3 : Books and Songs

Books and Songs

Granny Wisdom did not spare anything when it came to cooking a meal. She always went all out. This night was no exception. She cooked fried chicken, mashed potatoes with gravy, green beans and large, plump, hot rolls covered in butter.

Ran ate while Granny Wisdom recounted the day to his grandfather. She got especially excited when she mentioned meeting Katie.

"Randall, she is a pretty girl, and they just talked and talked. I saw her over with her girlfriends, looking at Ran, and I even told him as much, but he didn't believe me. We even know her parents, Don and Betty Summers. They go to my church—well, Betty still does; I think they are separated now . . . a pity. Anyhow, that means she must go to church, too. I have never seen her there, but you know how our church has grown, and the youth are always having their meetings."

Granny Wisdom stopped talking and made a sound like someone makes when they forget something important. "Oh, Ran, I forgot to tell you. Pastor Westerfield wants you to play your guitar and sing a special tomorrow morning."

The news startled Ran. He felt like someone had shot a hole straight through him.

"What? No! I can't—I mean I don't know all those people." He imagined Katie watching him sing, and the feeling of bees inside his stomach returned.

The professor cleared his throat. "Remember how your grandmother paid for your lessons when you were young? This will be a way to pay her back."

Granny Wisdom interrupted, "Oh, don't do it for that reason, Ran. Do it because you want to."

Ran stayed up late Saturday night, tuning his guitar and practicing several songs. Sunday morning came quickly, and he even practiced singing in the shower.

When he and Granny pulled up to the church, Ran was shocked. The Arkadelphia Family Church was nothing like he remembered. His father's church used to be in a small, brick building, and they only had around sixty members. According to Granny Wisdom, that church building was torn down and replaced by a large metal building, which sat 200 members. To Ran's surprise, the church presently held two Sunday morning services, putting their attendance at 320. The growth was mostly due to a large increase in teen-agers and college students.

Ran couldn't help but think about the time he and the deacon's son skipped Sunday School to play war. They wound up in a terrible fist fight, which ended with Ran getting a spanking and a lecture when he got home.

People were outside the church, milling about, visiting, when a bell rang, indicating Sunday School was to begin. Granny Wisdom juggled three boxes of doughnuts in one hand. Finally Ran asked if he could help. She gave him one to take to his class.

"I can handle the rest," she said. "Hurry to class. We don't want you to be late."

He walked into Sunday School, placed the doughnuts on a table, sat in the back row, and tried to be invisible. He was not feeling sociable this particular morning.

A tall, skinny man with a large, hooked nose walked to the front of the class. He was dressed casually for a church setting, Ran thought. But nowadays, people dressed more casually in the States when going to church. The tall man had on Capri pants, sandals and a cabana shirt. Ran thought the guy looked like he belonged in Mexico instead of Arkansas. Ran took his Bible out of his leather carrying bag, and in his bag he found his home school textbooks— the same ones he had picked up two weeks earlier . . . the very day his dad was killed.

On second glance, Ran noticed that they were not actually books, but boxes shaped like books. There were three of them, and on the outside cover of the boxes was a holographic picture of an angel, which appeared to move his sword when Ran moved the box. The first box was titled "Old Testament Survey: Four Adventures in Time."

"What a strange title," Ran mumbled to himself.

The second box had the same hologram on the front and was titled "New Testament Survey: Jesus and The Early Church." Ran looked at the third box and thought it was as strange as the others. It was titled "Church History: Men of Reformation."

Ran was most puzzled by the boxes that were shaped to look like books. "I wonder what's inside," Ran whispered as he tore open the Old Testament Survey box. He peered inside to discover a CD-ROM disk. "Oh, an interactive textbook," Ran mumbled to himself.

Ran looked up and saw that almost everyone in the room was staring at him. He quickly put the boxes back in his black leather bag.

The tall, hook-nosed man smiled at him and spoke in what seemed a genuinely kind voice. "Hello. We have a new student with us this morning, and it appears he even brought doughnuts. How nice."

Ran could not help but stare at the man's nose while replying, "They're from my grandmother, Jane Wisdom."

"Oh, you must be their grandson, Randall, Junior. Well, Randy, it is good to have you join us. My name is Paul Preacher. I know what you are thinking: 'Paul Preacher is my Sunday School teacher'."

But that was not what Ran was thinking at all. He was thinking, "How dare you call me Randy? "

"It's Ran."

"Pardon?" Paul looked puzzled.

"My name. I go by Ran, not Randy. It's just . . . my mom always called me Ran, and I prefer it to Randy."

Paul seemed embarrassed, "Oh, I am so sorry. Class, you should also note that Ran just moved here from the Philippines, where his dad, our former pastor, Reverend James Wisdom, joined the heavenly—"

Don't say it, please don't. Ran swallowed a gallon of anger.

Preacher continued his sentence, "—as a martyr. Yes, his father gave his life for the highest—"

Ran tried to hide his anger as he interrupted Paul Preacher again, "Indonesia! We lived in Indonesia." He looked around and saw a few of the youth group looking at him as if they felt sorry, though the majority just looked nervous.

"Well, anyhow, Randy—I mean Ran—we are glad to have you here. Please thank your grandmother for the doughnuts." Paul Preacher went on to teach the class about Samson and Delilah. He asked them not to fall into temptation this school year and risk losing their anointing.

The lesson would have been more enjoyable to Ran if his head hadn't been set on fire with anger. Instead of listening, Ran was mostly trying to figure out why this big-nosed guy, who probably just graduated from Bible school, had gone and exposed the most private aspect of his life to a room of total strangers. Ran felt like he might as well have come to church in his underwear.

The bell finally rang again, and Ran tried to slip out to go get his guitar when he saw Katie Summers at the table near the door eating a doughnut. He tried to act like he did not see her as he went through the door, hoping to avoid further embarrassment.

"Hi, stranger," Katie said, popping up in front of his face.

"Hi. You didn't happen to arrive late for class, did you?" Ran asked.

"No, but don't worry. I think Pastor Preacher could have exercised a little more grace when he introduced you."

"Is he the pastor of the church now?"

"No, silly, he's our youth pastor. Crazy name, huh? A preacher named Preacher." Katie hit him on the arm and smiled. He felt dizzy as he looked at her hair and smelled her perfume. She was dressed in a pink dress. But of course he was not interested in girls. He was interested in football, school, and music.

"MUSIC! I've got to go to . . . 'bye."

He was supposed to meet the worship leader after Sunday School. Ran took off in a dash. Katie stared, puzzled, as he went out the door.

Ran sat at the back corner of the stage in the sanctuary, tuning his guitar, while six young adults gathered for a meeting. He assumed they were the worship team.

The sanctuary filled up quickly and Brian Mecklenburg, the staff worship leader, spoke quietly to the worship team, occasionally glancing over his shoulder at Ran.

As they met, Ran tried to think of something to say to the church before singing his special. He really did not feel spiritual lately. In fact, he doubted God more now than ever. One of his biggest fears was his home church discovering the doubts in his heart and disappointing those who knew his father.

The sanctuary was full before service began, and to everyone's surprise a large crowd had gathered outside, waiting for ushers to find them a seat. Not long after, Pastor Westerfield asked the ushers to let the crowd in to stand if they desired. One of the ushers had an idea for the altar to be removed and replaced with three more rows of seats. Pastor Westerfield approved the idea and announced to the congregation that the service would start fifteen minutes late.

Ran was concerned. He approached the music leader. "Excuse me, sir. Why are there so many people coming to today's service?"

Mecklenburg smiled, "Don't you know?"

"No."

"It's because of you. Everyone wants to hear about what happened in Indonesia. You're big news."

Ran's face went numb like a five-ton bucket of ice water had been poured over him.

The pastor approached the microphone and said, "I would like Ran Wisdom to come forward."

Ran wasn't listening.

"Ran, good morning!" The pastor waved.

Sweat gathered in beads across Ran's top lip, and his neck was stiff as a two-by-four. He was in shock.

"I was wondering if you could come forward and share your song and if you would like to give your testimony."

Ran had always liked Pastor Westerfield, but at the moment the pastor was like a two-horned demon. Nevertheless, he walked up to the microphone and looked out at the congregation, who stared back at him—some with encouraging smiles, others with sympathetic, weepy eyes, but all of it made Ran sick. He was the variety show, the spectator sport, the story of the hour.

He could hear a few whisper how they always liked him, though they barely knew him. Most of them knew his father, and when they saw Ran, they saw his dad. Some of them remembered him from his childhood. He had respect from his elders that he had never earned, which made him uncomfortably self-conscious. He feared that he eventually would disappoint them.

"Good morning." The microphone squealed briefly. He cleared his throat. "First, I would like to thank Pastor Westerfield for asking me to sing. Brother Westerfield was my father's associate pastor before we left for Indonesia— and my father always said good things about you." Ran looked at the pastor.

Westerfield smiled.

Looking back at the packed auditorium, Ran continued, "As many of you know, I just returned from Indonesia. And, as I am sure you are aware, my father, James Wisdom, did not make it back home with me. He was murdered." A few people in the audience gasped.

One lady, Ely Bligh, who was known for dramatics, called out, "Bless you, child, we love you."

Ran continued, "I am, it seems, a survivor of terror— terror inflicted by Muslim extremists. Terrorist attacks are something I became quite used to in Jakarta, Indonesia. I didn't think it would ever happen to my family, though. I guess that's the way a lot of Americans felt last year during 9/11. I can definitely understand. I know firsthand what loss is like."

Ran searched for words. "Apostle Paul said to be absent from this body is to be present with the Lord. That's the scripture I've been thinking about since I lost my dad. He is in a better place. I know that still doesn't answer all of our questions about death, but if you came this morning looking for answers, there is Someone you can turn to who has the answers."

As Ran was speaking, many in the congregation were crying for the loss of their former pastor. Sister Bligh raised her white hanky high and waved it back and forth.

Ran was nervous. "The song that I am going to sing this morning is about a Man who knew suffering. In fact, when His best friend, Lazarus, died, the Bible says He wept. Right now that Man is here today. He knows your fears and my fears. He's the only one we can put our trust in today. As I sing this song, He wants to minister to you. His name is Jesus."

Ran sang his song, and many people raised their hands as tears rolled down their cheeks. Some bowed their heads in silence, and others held the hand of someone close to them.

When Ran was finished, he put down his guitar. The last few minutes were a blur. Did he really go into that long speech?

The thoughts in the minds of many in the church this particular morning were clear. They were all asking themselves, "Who was Ran Wisdom?" And many had the feeling that he was going to be someone special one day.

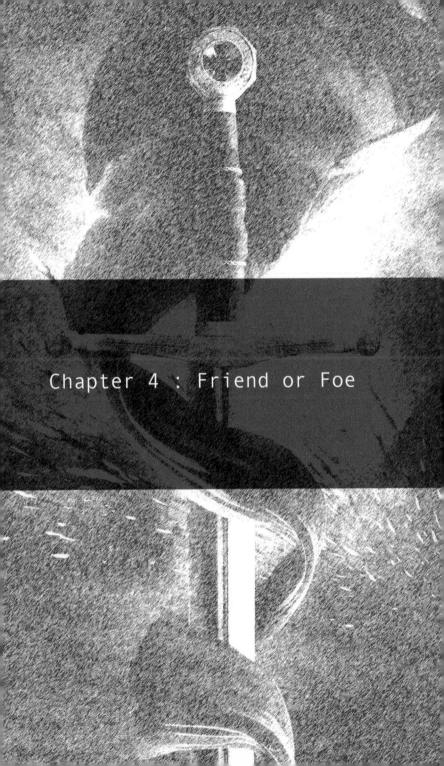

Chapter 4 : Friend or Foe

Friend or Foe

After the service was over, several members welcomed Ran back to Arkadelphia. Many people he did not know consoled him for the loss of his father. He did not get a chance to talk with Katie afterwards, and by this time he was regretting his behavior in Sunday School. Lately his temper was a short fuse.

As Ran was waiting for his grandmother by the car, Pastor Preacher approached, grinning widely and arms opened wide.

"You are a blessing," Preacher exclaimed, as he wrapped his arms around Ran in a bear hug. An awkward long hug, of which Ran felt relieved to be set loose.

"Look here," Preacher said wisely, "Coming back home is going to be hard. I'm sure you are quite angry from all that has happened. . . You know, everything happens for a reason, I mean who knows why God sends us these trials? Right? I mean, 'His ways are higher than our ways', right?"

Ran knew the chapter and verse, but the words didn't feel right. A voice inside Ran seemed to whisper, "Right words sometimes are wrong."

Ran shook off the thought, hoping his grandmother would soon return. She must still be visiting with friends, he thought.

"Look here, Ran," Pastor Preacher continued, "Right now you are lost. You are going to need a father figure. More than anything you need a covering. I know I am just a lowly youth pastor, in your eyes. I mean, compared to your father, I must not seem like a big deal, right?"

By this point, Ran didn't care what this guy was blubbering on about. . . but Preacher continued, none the less.

"So, that's what I believe God put me here to do. To be

your 'covering'." Preacher used his fingers like quotation marks. "You good with that?"

Just then a voice came from behind Pastor Preacher, and it was about time, too. It was Granny Wisdom.

"Hello, Pastor Preacher," Granny hugged Preacher. "Glad to see you young men hanging out here together. I hope I didn't keep you waiting too long?"

"Noooooo," Preacher patted Ran on the back aggressively. "By no means."

Preacher held out his hand toward Granny with a grand gesture, "I mean look here Ran, who else has a grandmother named wisdom? This boy is all kinds of blessed!"

Hours later, in his bedroom, Granny's roast beef and boiled potatoes rested heavily on Ran's stomach as he lay in bed. He was thinking about the speech he had made at church. He had said things in front of over five hundred people that he would not say to his grandparents. His dad always told him a man knows he is called to preach when he can get up on a stage, forget about everything else in his life and speak with conviction. However, Ran did not want to be in the ministry anymore. To give a speech and sing a song occasionally was one thing, but to allow himself to come to his father's end was another.

Ran was also pondering the strange encounter with the youth pastor. Something strange was happening there, and he couldn't put his finger on it.

His mind then wandered to Katie. What a coincidence running into her and then her coming to church. A smile played across his lips as he drifted off into some foggy and soon forgotten dream. It was something about the future. Something about Katie. Something about a white wedding dress. . .

He was almost asleep when the phone rang and scared him so badly he jerked up and hit his head. Granny Wisdom opened the study room door, holding the phone out toward him.

"Randall, Jr., are you all right? The phone call is for you."

"Yes, I'm fine. Thank you." Ran took the phone and rubbed his aching head. "Hello."

"Ran, guess who this is?"

Ran checked his head to see if he was bleeding and answered, "I don't know. Who is it?"

"It's me, fool, Gray Floyd! You sound like you're in pain. Are they horsewhipping you over there? Just tell me and I'll come wrestle the professor down while you take on old Granny."

Ran was excited to hear a familiar voice. "No, I just hit my stupid head. Ouch!"

They both laughed. "I've been thinking about you. How did you know I was back in town?"

"Easy. Katie calls my house every ten minutes since I gave in and said I'd be her boyfriend."

The news hit Ran like a fist to the jaw, so he lay back down on the couch, forgetting about the pain in his head, for now the pain seemed to have moved straight to his heart.

"Oh, I didn't realize you two were going out. I mean, she didn't say anything to me." Ran did not want Gray to know he had a crush on his best friend's girlfriend. No, not a crush. Ran did not like her. He liked football and music. Not girls.

Not that he didn't "like" girls. Every boy likes girls,

but girls are a distraction and in Ran's experience a huge annoyance.

What was he thinking? It was probably Grandma's cooking and the last few weeks messing with his emotions. Anyhow, he did not want Gray to think he. . . liked her.

"Well, I wanted to go out with Grace Moore, but she's crazy about Jude Tripp."

Ran recalled the name Jude Tripp. "I met that jerk in town."

"What do you mean 'jerk?' He happens to be my best friend and the quarterback of the team."

Ran closed his eyes and could not ignore the pain in his head any longer. "Well, I don't know who you're hanging out with these days, but he acted like a jerk the other day when I met him."

"He probably just saw you talking to Katie and wanted to stick up for me."

Ran changed the subject. "Oh, maybe he's not so bad, then. Hey, so you are on the football team?"

"Yeah, I got picked for first string receiver. Hey, how would you like to go to a party at Jude's house? His dad's loaded. I think they made all their money in Texas before the oil market dropped out in the '80s. They have an indoor swimming pool and everything. So do you want to go or what?"

"I don't know, Gray. Tonight's a school night, and Granny will never let me leave the house. Besides, how will we get there?"

"Don't worry about how we'll get there, and don't tell your grandparents you're coming—just sneak out. I'll come by at eleven, and you can meet me at the corner where the oak tree used to be."

Ran recalled the oak tree where the professor had built

a tree house. A long time ago, Gray would come over and they would spend all night out there. The tree had been hit by lightning last summer and removed.

"I don't think this is a good idea. How will we get to the party? I don't have enough money for cab fare."

"I told you. Don't worry about that. I have us covered. Come on, Ran, this is your chance to meet some girls and get to know some people. It wouldn't hurt to loosen up a little, or did you get too righteous at church this morning? Katie told me how you preached or something."

Ran gave in to the pressure. "Okay, I'll go. Just promise me we won't get caught."

Ran paced up and down the street, waiting at the corner where the old oak tree used to stand. He was now regretting he had agreed to go to the party. He and Gray used to think parties were stupid. Obviously Gray had changed since he left. Just how much was still to be known.

Ran was looking for Gray to come walking up the street or riding his bike; instead he drove up on a red dirt bike.

"Get on the back and hold on tight."

"Where did you get this?" Ran asked.

"It's my older brother's. Don't worry—he lets me take it out whenever I want. Besides, his girlfriend's over, so he's a little preoccupied."

"What about your parents? Where are they?"

Gray laughed, "Like they care what I do anymore. My dad lives in Houston now, and Mom works nights at the hospital."

Ran felt embarrassed. "I'm sorry. No one told me your

parents divorced."

"Don't be sorry, dude. It's the best thing that ever happened. I get to do whatever I want, and, once a month, I get to go to Houston, where I have two other girlfriends. The coolest thing is none of them knows about the others."

Ran looked at the dirt bike. "I know you're not old enough to drive this thing."

"Quit being such a prude, and get on the bike."

Ran reluctantly got on the bike. Not only was Gray different, he was a good-for-nothing two-timer, and Katie Summers could do much better.

The ride to Jude's house took half an hour, and, by the time they arrived, Ran's backside was numb. They got off the bike and walked up a steep driveway leading to a tall, iron gate. Gray reached over to the intercom in the bushes and pushed a button.

"The password is 'Let it all burn'."

A voice answered back, "Who's that with you?"

"This is Ran. He's cool."

"Oh, it's the foreigner. Why'd you bring him?"

"We used to be friends in the sixth grade, dummy; now let us in. I want some beer!"

The gate opened and Ran was sick. He didn't know he was going to a drinking party and felt naive. He tried to think of a way to leave, but had no idea how to get home if he found a ride. As they walked into the house, three tall guys in football jerseys whispered something into Gray's ear. Without a word, Gray exited the room with the three guys and left Ran standing in a room full of strangers.

What am I doing here?

From behind him he heard, "Hey, stranger!"

It was Katie, and she had obviously had a few drinks.

Katie stumbled over to Ran and said, "I know what

you're thinking: How can someone go to church on Sunday morning and get drunk on Sunday night? I know I am a hypocrite, but aren't we all? I mean, look at you. You were preaching this morning, and now you're here."

"Well, if it makes you feel any better, I wish I wasn't." Ran walked the other way.

"Wait a minute. No one walks off while I'm talking."

"What? Do you think you're special because you're pretty? Do you think you can blink your big eyes at me and make me feel all right about being called a hypocrite?"

"What's wrong with you? I was just . . . never mind."

Katie turned around and walked out the front door. Ran did not want her to be by herself outside, so he followed her.

"Katie, come here. I'm just—I'm just—"

"What?" she turned and locked eyes with him.

"I'm just mad that you didn't tell me you were going out with Gray."

Just then Jude walked up from the gate.

"Hey, Katie, is this guy bugging you again? You need me to handle him?"

Jude pushed his chest up against Ran's and stared up into his face, breathing a foul stench of liquor into Ran's nostrils.

Ran was calm and relaxed. He tried to remember some of the martial arts training he had been taking from his friends in Indonesia. He centered himself. Jude pushed his face closer.

"You stink, dude," Ran said in a calm, matter-of-fact voice.

"What did you say to me?" Jude backed up and made a fist. Just then Katie came between them.

"Stop. Jude, let's go find Gray."

She grabbed Jude's hand and pulled him away. They

walked back into the house. Ran sat down on a bench outside.

Two hours later, Gray came outside.

"I've been looking for you. Do you want to go swim?"

"No. I think it's time to go."

Gray could see in Ran's razor-sharp glance that he meant business.

"Okay. Let me tell everyone we're leaving."

"One more thing, Gray—I am going to drive."

Ran was surprised that Gray didn't argue. They both knew Gray was too drunk to drive. On the way home, they did not talk except when Gray gave him directions. When they arrived at Ran's house, he got off the bike and looked at Gray.

"Well, it's late, and tomorrow's my first day at school."

"You don't have to explain. It was time to go," Gray said as he fiddled with his helmet.

"Are you going to be all right driving home?"

"Yeah, the trip back sobered me up."

"Are you sure?" Ran was worried. "Look, just sneak into my room and sleep on the floor."

"No. My brother doesn't mind me driving this thing, but he'd get ticked off if it's not in the garage by morning."

Ran felt awkward. "Well, it's been good seeing you again. I'll see you at school tomorrow."

They gave each other five, but both knew things were not the same.

Before Ran went to sleep, he remembered when he and Gray were playing football in the sixth grade for a Boys' Club team called the Lightning Bolts. Ran was the quarterback and Gray was the receiver. It was the final tournament, and they were down by three points. Just like a movie, only a few seconds remained on the clock. At the thirty-yard line, Ran received the hiked ball and dodged two tackles. A third boy, who was rather large, came running for him, and just then he saw Gray open in the end zone. He passed the ball just in time before being plowed over. When he looked up, Gray caught the ball and scored a touchdown. They had barely won. That same night, he and Gray stayed up talking about the game in the clubhouse of his grandfather's old oak tree. Those times were gone.

Ran longed for those days. Inside his heart he ached for anything resembling the past. But the past was just that . . . past.

He knelt down by his bed for the first time in awhile and he prayed. And in that prayer he said something that touched the very heart of God. He did not just think of his own needs, he thought of his friend Gray.

"Dear Lord, I ask you to help me to get some sleep tonight. God, I can tell that Gray needs you. Help me to be a light to him as he goes through this dark time in his life. Oh, God, one last thing: Help me get on the football team.

Chapter 5 : God Was Moved

God Was Moved

I was perched on top of the Wisdoms' roof, just above the study Ran called home. It was after he returned from the big party. I felt perplexed. The mission was more difficult than I had thought.

My orders from above were going to be difficult to carry out. I was supposed to take three ragtag teen-agers—Ran, Katie and Jude—and magically transform them into apostle, prophet, and teacher of this generation. On top of that, I was given special orders for Gray Floyd. He was what the report labeled "A Big Challenge." According to my orders, he was chosen to be the evangelist of the group. However, the orders made it clear that I was to focus much of my energy and time on the other three for now, and I had not even begun to work on Jill Denver.

I leaned my head down onto my arms in my lap and allowed my usually disciplined mind to wander. I am reluctant to admit it, but I was thinking about Chicago in the fall. In particular, I was thinking about the young boys in my old neighborhood assignment. They loved to play basketball. They lived for it. There was one boy in particular I was thinking about. His name was Gary. I saved Gary's life one night—not that I am bragging, but that was what I was thinking about. I was thinking about the feeling I had one night when I fought off three large spirits of death who were controlling a local drug pusher. The pusher was livid. He had had a large amount of drug money stolen. Angrily he rushed into the streets, looking for the thieves. The first person he saw was Gary. The mad man took Gary by the throat, mistaking him for a thief. He would have killed Gary had I not fought off the spirits of death.

The fight was intense—the worst ever for me. Finally they yielded, and the drug pusher suddenly came to his mind. His entire face changed. For a moment, his eyes were like an innocent child. He let Gary go and even apologized. The most amazing thing is that Gary would one day go on to play for the Chicago Bulls. I saved his life. It is a moment I am most fond of, I suppose.

Anyway, I was thinking about Gary and thanking God for creating me and giving me purpose. I was reminding myself that God did not place me in this position without giving me the means and strength to do the job.

That is when it happened: Wind began to blow. Not Arkansas wind—Holy Spirit wind. I recognized the feeling. Someone had touched the heart of God. My spirit filled with holy fire. It was God's breath upon my dry bones, giving me the strength I needed to fulfill my call.

I opened up a Bible I kept in my carry-on. The Lord spoke to me clearly to look at the book of Revelation. I read through several chapters.

At first I did not understand. "God, what are you trying to tell me?" I asked with desperation.

His answer came to my heart like clear creek water from the mountains: "Did John see the future?" God asked.

That is all, just one question. I began to ponder. The Lord was testing me, and I wanted very much to please my King. John was taken in a vision to see things to come, I thought.

Then I asked God the question that started me onto the trail that led to the next phase of my mission. I asked, "God, if John saw the future, can humans see the past?"

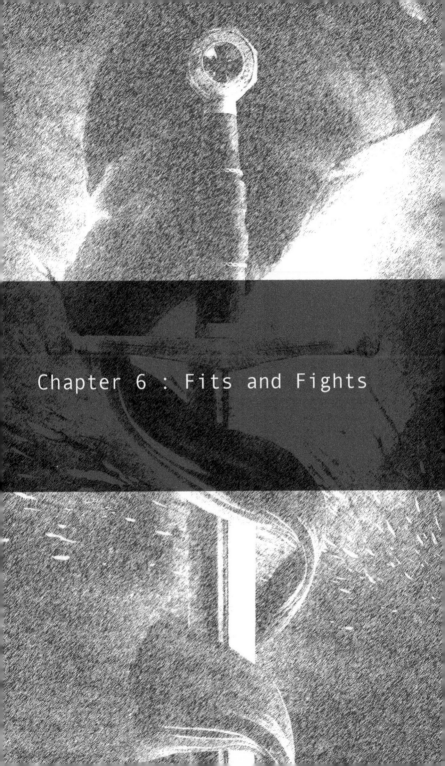

Chapter 6 : Fits and Fights

Fits and Fights

By the time the first bell rang, Ran was sitting in the counselor's office, filling out paper work. The counselor seemed most concerned about Ran's shot record. She said she did not want him spreading a foreign disease around the school. He was embarrassed, but understood her feelings. His mother had died from a rare blood infection that the doctors thought she had contracted on a summer Mexico mission.

The counselor radioed the nurse, asking her to come give him a physical. Ran's insides felt like mush. He had eaten little breakfast because of nerves, and as yet he had not seen Gray or Katie. While waiting for the nurse, the counselor asked him for his transcripts and standard achievement scores from last year. He opened his bag to discover he had his transcripts, which had his grades from the last two years, but he did not have his standardized test scores. He remembered the deacons of the church having these important papers, but could not remember if they had given them to him before he left Jakarta.

"Well?" From behind her desk, the counselor stared at him through thick spectacles. She was a large, Hispanic woman in her mid-forties. Her hair was long, thick and very dark. Ran could not tell if she was being rude or if she was just overworked.

"I don't have them. I can contact someone who does, and they can fax them to you." Ran answered.

"Well, you can't call Indonesia from a school phone, so you will need to call from home. After your physical, you might as well get someone to give you a ride home and make that call, because we cannot place you until we have those papers." She spoke quickly while typing at her computer without looking up.

Ran's first-day nerves were now completely gone. Instead he was angry. "What? I can't just go home." He was embarrassed to share his personal situation with a stranger, but had no choice. "I have no way home. My grandfather works all day and only has one car, so my grandmother can't come to get me."

The counselor looked up briefly through her glasses and her eyes looked big and scary. "Do you have a father or mother, Mr. Wisdom?"

Ran was indignant, "Yes. They are in heaven presently with the angels. Would you like me to try to get them on the phone, or would the school object to that long-distance call? The charge would probably be outrageous. Wait—I will get them to fly down from heaven, over to Jakarta, get my papers and drop them off." He knew he had gone too far and expected he would meet the principal shortly.

He was surprised at her reaction. "Mr. Wisdom, I am sorry." She looked concerned. "I did not realize. I apologize. I must seem very rude to you. I am actually trying to find a way to help you. You see, school policy states that any student who enters public school after attending home school must provide test results. The test results prove you are ready to go into the desired grade level. In other words, Mr. Wisdom, without those papers you will not be attending high school this year but will be held back. You will return to the eighth grade.

Ran went from feeling angry to appalled. "Miss, I made straight A's last year. Look at my report card." He handed her his transcript.

She stared at it through the thick lenses of her glasses. "Yes. Very good." She coughed into a handkerchief, looked up at him, and smiled. "You will not be happy to hear this,

Mr. Wisdom, but these grades are inconsequential. We have to see what you made on the standardized . . ."

Ran interrupted, "Yes, I know, the standardized achievement scores. Can I get a ride home?"

She returned his scowl with a smile. "Okay. After the nurse gives you a physical, you will receive a ride home from one of our custodial staff."

He sat in the office for another hour, listening to Mrs. Black type furiously. He joked to himself, "She is probably just writing e-mail."

"E-MAIL!" Ran yelled it so loud that Mrs. Black jumped and knocked her coffee mug onto the floor.

"Excuse me?" she asked while cleaning up the mess.

"I forgot. I could e-mail a few of my dad's friends who have the scores and they could send the scores. That way there is no charge for the phone call."

"You are very clever, Mr. Wisdom," she said, smiling. She invited Ran to her side of the desk and left the room, whistling. Ran e-mailed two deacons from his old church. He was feeling much better by the time the nurse came in to give him a physical.

After his physical, he was informed that one of the deacons, Missionary Jeff Rudy, had faxed his scores to the school. The counselor was surprised when she studied his scores. Not only was he on grade-level, but also was eligible for advanced courses. Ran smiled as he signed up for every advanced class offered.

"Where can I find the football coach?" Ran asked, after enrolling in his last class.

"Not so fast. You need books. Do you know where our book store is?"

"No." He was worried he needed money for the books. She read his mind.

"Don't worry, the books are paid for by the state, but we keep them in our book store. Since you don't know your way around campus, I will get you an escort."

She picked up her radio and called for an escort to be sent to her office.

Ran felt relieved to be leaving her office and almost forgot that she had not answered his question about the football coach. "Mrs. Black, thank you for your help this morning." He reached out his hand to shake hers. He was trying to make up for his former outbursts, but before she even noticed the gesture, the door opened and Jude Tripp walked in, grinning.

"You need me, Mrs. Black?" he croaked.

"Yes, Jude. This is Randall Wisdom, Jr. He likes to be called Ran. He needs you to show him to the book store and give him a tour around the campus to meet each of his teachers. He won't be starting class until tomorrow. Oh, yes, since you're on the football team, he also wants to meet Coach Jordan. You can introduce him." She glanced at Jude with a smile, peered through her glasses and proudly announced, "Jude is our star quarterback."

Jude waited outside, which was fine with Ran. A half-hour later, Jude walked Ran around the school, neither of them talking. Jude just grunted as he pointed out his classrooms.

First, Ran met Mrs. Kraush, his Advanced Algebra teacher. She was a short, thin woman, who primped her gray hair as they talked outside her room. She seemed glad to meet him.

"I am always glad to meet gifted students," she said as she shook his hand. Ran was surprised to learn from Mrs. Kraush that while he had been in the book store, Mrs. Black, the counselor, had already walked around to each of his teachers and shown them his standardized test scores.

Next Ran met his Advanced Earth Science teacher, Mr. Blackhurst. He was a tall, bald, black man, with a round belly and a jolly disposition.

"You won't be disappointed this year, Ran. I promise to challenge you to your limits. I do not give away easy A's. In fact, last year, no one made an A." He chuckled to himself as if he had told a very funny joke, but Ran didn't get it.

After that, he met the Advanced English teacher, Mrs. Landes. She was a tall, beautiful brunette, who had just graduated from graduate school. He was embarrassed to talk to her because she was so beautiful. She was excited and animated as she talked. She seemed a little too excited to be teaching. Ran thought it might be because she was new.

As Jude and Ran walked to his next class, Jude finally acknowledged Ran and said, "What did you think of Mrs. Landes?"

Ran knew very well what he meant, but did not want to let him know that he thought she was a living goddess. A real Helen of Troy, he thought, but not out loud. No, he just smiled and replied, "She's all right."

"All right?" What's wrong with you, dude? You got something for guys? Oh, yeah, maybe I'll take you down to the Theatre. That's where your kind hangs out."

Offended at the small-mindedness of Jude, Ran quipped, "First of all, if you look on my schedule, I am taking Drama this year, and if you had half a brain, you would realize that acting is only for the gifted and talented students. However, people like you always have to punish those who intimidate you. I guess brains aren't your strong suit."

Jude crumbled Ran's schedule and tossed it into a trash can. "If you're so smart, find your own way around the school, loser. And, by the way, I already had a little talk with Coach Jordan, and he said the team's not taking foreigners or orphans."

Ran's face dropped. His mind was blank.

Jude did not stop, "Don't cry, Little Orphan Annie. Why don't you go home and read Oliver Twist or rent Good Will Hunting? Maybe we can call Robin Williams in for a little therapy. 'Oh, please feel sorry for me, everyone. I live with my granny.' Oh, I didn't mention, Wisdom, it seems we have one thing in common: We both are in advanced classes. So I will see you in every period of the day—except for when you're kissing on the boys in Drama class, of course. Smoochy, smoochy."

Before Ran even realized what he was doing, his fist hit Jude's mid-section, knocking out his air. Ran used all of his strength to hit Jude again—this time across the mouth, blood spilling out on the white tile floor.

Jude jumped up, outraged at the sight of his own blood. He gained his breath and charged for Ran, but Ran turned quickly, causing Jude to run directly into the trash can. Ran raced over, grabbed Jude by the collar, dug in the trash can and pulled out his schedule.

"I think you still owe me a tour of three more classes, you imbecile." Just then, Ran looked up and noticed the hall was full of gazing spectators. Behind a group of students stood a tall, white-haired man in a black suit and tie. Ran figured out quickly that he had just met Principal Williams.

Pat Williams, the principal of Arkadelphia High School, was usually a man of great intelligence—at least Ran thought so. When he spoke, one must listen carefully, for he spoke so intelligently that no one was sure what he had said—sometimes not even him.

Ran sat in his office alone, waiting for him. Looking around the room, no one could miss the trophies which lined the shelves. They were debate trophies, and there must have been fifty or sixty of them. Obviously to Ran, Mr. Williams was once a great debate coach before he became a principal.

The door slowly opened, and, before the man entered, his long shadow fell on the floor in front of Ran, making Ran's stomach jump into his chest. Mr. Williams walked in long, slow strides towards his desk, but stopped at a shelf and picked up one of his trophies.

In a deep, Southern accent, Mr. Williams asked, "Do you know what this is, Mr. Wisdom?" He did not wait for a reply. "This is a Louisiana State University debate trophy that one of my top students won at a state tournament. The topic he was given to debate was 'High School Violence.' He was asked to take the affirmative and persuade judges on how high school violence could be prevented." He looked away from the trophy and into Ran's eyes. "Do you know what he said, Mr. Wisdom? He said that high school principals should expel students at their first violation. He suggested a no-nonsense policy. 'Send them all a message' is what he said. He won the debate, Mr. Wisdom."

A long pause followed. Mr. Williams put the trophy back on the shelf. Meanwhile Ran was trying to figure out how to tell his grandparents that he was expelled on the first day of school.

"Mr. Wisdom, I disagree with the argument."

Ran relaxed a bit.

Principal Williams continued, "You see, if I expel you, both of us lose. You lose an opportunity to attend a great school, and I lose a brilliant young man. Now, on the other hand, if I did expel you, it would send a message to every student that I take fighting seriously—and I do. But, you see, I would rather send another message. The message that I want the student body to receive is mercy. If I return violence with violence, does that cancel everything out? No, it does not. But if I give you both another chance that says that I stand against fighting but I also stand for mercy, the responsibility is on me to be the peacemaker here. Now, with that said, I give you a warning: Fighting solves nothing. If you start out this way at Arkadelphia High, you'll end up fighting every student that provokes you. Now, do you want to spend your years here like that?"

Somewhere in the lecture, Ran got completely lost. The principal wanted an answer, and Ran was confused about the question, so he said, "Excuse me, Mr. Williams, could you repeat the question?"

"Hmm, I guess so. Let's see, where was I?" He rubbed his nose. "Oh, yes, I was asking you not to fight anymore."

"Oh, yes, sir. I will not fight anymore. I don't know what got into me. I promise not to do it again."

Mr. Williams walked over to his desk and said, "Good— very good." He leaned toward Ran and said, "Mr. Wisdom, two students saw what happened in the hall. They informed me that Mr. Tripp called you a few names. Next time this happens, you come to me. Well, why are you sitting there, son? You are free to go with a warning. I hope the next time I see you in my office, it is on better terms. Good day!" Before Ran left, Mr. Williams called after him again, "Oh, Ran, this is your warning. You only get one. After this, if you fight, I will resort to the advice of my champion debate student and will expel you. Good day."

The door closed behind him, and Ran felt somewhat relieved. When walking out of Principal Williams' office, Ran spied Jude, waiting on the bench by the secretary, holding a wash-cloth to his mouth. He was next to talk to the principal.

Standing outside the office was Katie. "So you got to meet Mr. Williams. What did he do—put you in time out?"

"How did you know I was here?"

"Are you kidding?" Katie flipped her hair on her other shoulder and smiled, "It seems you are very popular now. Well, not so much with the football team, but with everyone who hates Jude—which is anyone not on the football team. Everyone loves to see someone stand up to the bully. I won't be surprised if they elect you class president."

Ran smiled.

Katie grabbed Ran's hand and pulled him down the hall a few steps before letting go.

"Actually I am here for a reason. Come with me—the counselor said you didn't finish your tour. Unfortunately, you are going to have to sit through the next class, because I am in the class, too, and our teachers said I can't miss."

Ran was puzzled. "Teachers? How many teachers are there?"

"Two. It's called team teaching. It's something new the school is trying."

"Oh, really? Which course is it?"

"World Cultures: Part One"

"Do you mean there is a Part Two?"

"They didn't tell you? This is a three-year progressive course. Like math, it is supposed to get harder every year."

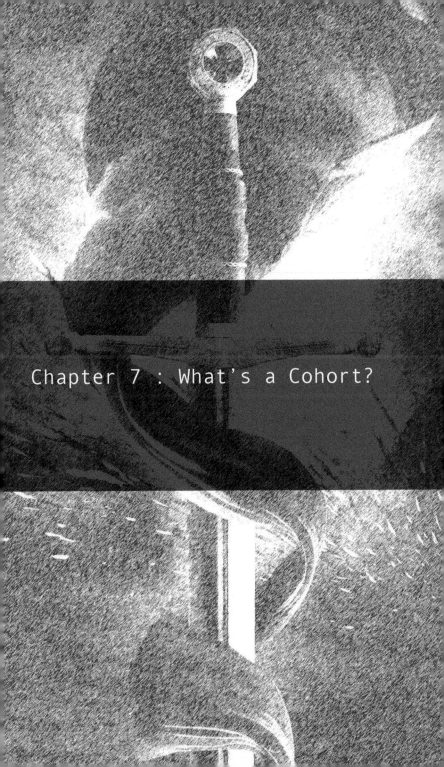

Chapter 7 : What's a Cohort?

What's a Cohort?

When Katie opened the door, Ran saw two male teachers at the front of the classroom. One had shoulder-length hair and was sitting on his desk dressed somewhat casually, and the other man was standing up front, lecturing. He had short, dark hair and was wearing a bow tie and a gray, pin-striped, three-piece suit without the jacket, making the vest look comical to Ran.

Ran whispered to Katie, "Who's this geek with the bow tie?"

"Ms. Summers, please inform the new student—" he looked at a paper on the desk "—Mr. Randall Wisdom, Jr., that we do not talk in this class unless given permission. My name is Professor Dr. Gaylord Douglas. You will call me Dr. Douglas or Professor Douglas, but never by my first name. Is that understood?"

He cleared his throat and straightened his bow tie as Ran and Katie sat down.

"Now, class, where was I? Oh, yes, today we are forming cohort groups. For those who are late coming in, cohort groups are made up of three students. Whatever group you are placed in, you will remain with your group for the next three years. You will be assigned a world culture to study, and every four weeks you will turn in a research paper which you have collaboratively written. Then you will take turns teaching the class what you have learned. At the end of every semester we will hold a debate, arguing as to which World Culture is superior and most influential in today's world. Professor Prichard and I will decide who will work best together, but, before we create your cohort group, we must first take out our textbooks and update ourselves as to what cultures are available for study."

Just as Ran was opening his book bag, his chair was

bumped from behind, making his books fly out all over the floor. It was Jude Tripp.

"Oops." Jude laughed as he sat down.

Professor Douglas smiled, "Mr. Tripp, nice to have you back."

Ran was picking up his books when he noticed the long-haired teacher he had not yet met bending down to help him pick them up.

The teacher met Ran's eyes, and, smiling, he stuck out his hand to greet him. "Rambo Prichard's my name." He then whispered, "I would let you call me Rambo, but Professor Douglas might get bent out of shape."

"I'm Ran Wisdom. Nice to meet you."

Mr. Prichard reached down and picked up one of Ran's books. He was staring at it while Ran began to gather up the rest.

Mr. Prichard read the title out loud: "Old Testament Survey: Four Adventures in Time."

"Oh, here, give me that. I am sorry, that's not supposed to be in my bag. I must have left it there."

"One second." Mr. Prichard was amused. He turned the box over and read to himself:

"Old Testament Survey: Four Adventures In Time. Like no other textbook, this interactive CD-ROM will lead students into four Old Testament adventures. First, the adventure begins with the Garden of Eden, where students will learn about how mankind chose their own will over God's. Secondly, students will venture on to see the near destruction of mankind when a flood covers the earth. The only one spared will be Noah's family and all land-dwelling animals. The third story will introduce Moses. They will learn how the children of Israel became slaves to the Egyptian Pharaoh. The student will rejoice with Israel and their victorious release from slavery and will learn why God made the Ten Commandments. They will witness Moses lead the people toward the Promised Land and through the desert, where Israel experienced many miracles. They will also see how the Israelites were then led into the promised land, called Canaan, by a leader named Joshua. The students will learn how the young generation procured the land promised to their forefather Abraham by God."

"In the fourth story, they will meet a great king named David, but they will meet him before he is a king, when he was just a shepherd. They will learn how much David went through to become a great King and they will also learn the mystery of the throne of David."

"These four stories will help the student learn the history and events that took place before the coming of Jesus. The student can interact with the textbook by clicking on an icon that looks like an angel, named Theta. The icon will answer questions and lead the student to scriptures related to topics."

Mr. Prichard handed the box back to Ran and walked up front to Professor Douglas. He and Douglas talked in whispers for a few moments as Ran gathered his books and sat down.

"Mr. Wisdom," Professor Douglas motioned Ran to come to the front of the room, "bring that CD and come up front—oh, yes, and bring Ms. Summers and Mr. Tripp with you."

Professor Douglas cleared his throat, straightened his bow tie and took the CD from Ran's hand. He took out his reading glasses and briefly read the back cover.

"Uh-huh. Mr. Wisdom, Professor Prichard has come up with a good idea. This textbook on CD would make a great study of a World Culture. I assume you know which culture I refer to—the Christian Culture. Mr. Wisdom, because this class studies world cultures, we are allowed to let you study religions, as long as we allow every religion a chance to be studied. We are going to allow you to use this as your text for research if you would like to study your religion's history. You will note that I personally think most of the stories of your people are no truer than Greek mythology."

He cleared his throat and straightened his tie again—a nervous habit, Ran thought. Mr. Prichard interrupted Dr. Douglas before he had a chance to expound. "Because of federal law concerning church and state, we are not allowed to advance your religion or inhibit it, so this is your choice, Ran. In regard to cohort groups, we want you, Katie and Jude to be on a team."

"What?" Ran blurted.

Professor Douglas raised his eyebrows and whispered through clenched teeth, "Mr. Wisdom, you will not question your authorities. We know about the incident between you and Mr. Tripp, and what better way to resolve your differences than to be on a team together?"

Katie looked at the CD-ROM box. "So if this is what we are studying this semester, then what about next semester and the next two years?"

Mr. Prichard seemed to have this covered. "If I'm not mistaken, Ran had several of these boxes in his bag. Is that right?"

Ran opened his bag, "Well, actually I have two other boxes. One is the Old Testament Survey, you already saw. One is New Testament Survey, and the last one looks like it is about Church history."

Dr. Douglas picked them each up, as if they were someone's dirty socks. "Yesssss, I see. Well, as long as we stay within the boundaries of school law, Lord knows I'm not sticking my neck out for you three. Remember though, the point is that several different points of view are going to be expounded upon. That means you will be hearing from the other groups about Buddhism, Islam, and several Native tribe beliefs. The point here is not to make all of us become Christians, the point is to thoroughly learn several world cultures. Do you understand?"

The bell rang and the classroom emptied. Katie was the only one left except Ran. She smiled and said, "We still have two classes for you to see, but, to tell you the truth, I really need to go get ready for volleyball practice."

"That's fine. I'm sure I'll manage to find them tomorrow," Ran replied.

The day was over, except one thing still remained: He had not yet talked to Coach Jordan.

Chapter 8 : New Friend/New Enemy

New Friend/New Enemy

The temperature outside was 97 degrees, and beads of sweat rolled down Ran's face as he walked toward the football field. Coach Jordan was to be meeting the team on the field soon, and if Ran hurried, he could get there before everyone else. Fortunately, when he arrived, the team was still dressing out in the field house, providing him with a few minutes to talk to the coach.

Ran approached slowly, as he built his faith with a scripture. "I can do all things through Christ who strengthens me!

"Excuse me?" Coach Jordan, a broad-shouldered man who once played for the Dallas Cowboys, turned around, staring at Ran.

"Hello, Coach. I'm Ran Wisdom. I just moved here and was wondering—"

"You're Randall Wisdom's grandson."

"You know my grandfather?" Ran stammered.

"I'm taking his night class. Yep, trying to add Physics to my teaching license. I had his class last Friday in fact. He said you'd want to talk to me. You want to be on the team?"

"Yes, sir! More than anything."

"Can you still throw the ball?"

"I practiced every day with my dad for the last two years." Ran smiled proudly.

"Well, I am going to take off running, and you're going to throw this ball to me." Coach Jordan tossed Ran a football and took off running down the field.

Ran did not think twice. He watched the coach give him a signal to throw and waited.

"What are you waiting for, boy?"

"You didn't go out far enough." Ran answered.

The coach laughed. Twenty more yards out he turned around, and Ran launched the ball in a perfect spiral, landing directly to target.

"Pretty good, pretty good." Coach jogged back up the field toward Ran. "Can you do it under pressure?"

"I guess you will have to let me try out," Ran said.

Chapter 9 : What Lies Beneath

What Lies Beneath

In the deepest, darkest part of a cold cave, beyond hearing ears, in a time long forgotten, a special meeting between two friends took place. A meeting not recorded in ancient text. A meeting that would forever start events to change the history of the Earth and the story of mankind.

On one side of the cave, an odd-looking snake with arms and legs stood tall, his face fixed in a contorted grin. He was smiling because he had waited six full moons to meet with his new friend, which he had decided was his new master. He even come to believe this friend to be his true father.

On the other side of the cave, in a dark corner, stood Snake's true father. The father of lies himself. The once covering cherub who was now cast down from among the stones of fire.

The ancient creature was draped in a long, black cloak with his face hidden well behind a hood. As he walked out of the shadows, he muttered, "Snake . . . Snake, hmm. I hate that name. There must be a better name for you. I guess Adam was running out of names when he got to you. Oh, don't look so down. I am merely saying you deserve a better name. Adam is the one to blame."

"Sssir, I am very excccited to sssee you. Did you call me here to tell me sssomething?" Snake bowed his head.

Walking toward Snake, the cloaked figure whispered, "You were supposed to be the King of Beasts—you, Snake, not Lion. Did you know that I am your father, your creator? But you seemed to have wandered far from me, bowing like a coward before that being you call Adam.

"Your mother before you, I called Wazet. A powerful being to this day. But you, I simply call Aalok, meaning light of god. You have been born to bring the light of truth, my truth to this world."

Snake grinned wildly. The stories his mother told him were all true and now he sat at the feet of his true father. Snake slithered down to all fours and curled around his master's legs. "What do you want, massster?"

"Hmm? The question is: Do you want, Aalok—do you want to live up to the stature of your new name?"

"I don't underssstand, massster."

"Really, Aalok, you being the most cunning creature in the Garden, one would think you would understand." He grabbed Snake gently by the face and pulled him up. "Look at me, son. Your destiny is to be King of Beasts. Adam made a drastic mistake." Snake smiled. "You must take your rightful place."

"But, massster, I cannot fight Lion. I may be more cunning, but I am not ssstronger," Snake replied as he lowered his head.

With a firm voice, the cloaked creature spoke, "It's not Lion you will overcome. You will go to the real source of your problems. You must remove the true obstacle: Adam."

"Oh, no, massster, not the chosen one. The Great Almighty One will not allow it."

"I AM THE GREAT ALMIGHTY ONE!" His voice cracked like thunder, Snake scurried to an opening in the cave to escape.

"Come back, Aalok." Calming himself, Snake's master walked to where Snake lay shivering. He rubbed his hand over Snake's head. "How are you going to become the new king of my kingdom?"

Snake thought for a moment. "The tree? Yesss, the tree. I will trick them into eating from the tree of Knowledge of Good and Evil."

Clapping his hands beneath the cloak, the creature hissed, "Very clever, my son."

Excitedly, Snake exclaimed, "Thank you, massster. I will go now. The day is cool. The chosen one will be almossst finissshed walking with—you know, the one who is not my massster."

"Well," said the cloaked one, "I commission you to go and take the place intended for you in my kingdom." He placed his ice-cold palm on Snake's back, escorting him out of the cave. At the entrance, Snake's master stopped. "I must go now back to my palace. I promise you: When you return, I will have your throne ready next to mine." With a push, Snake wandered out of the gloomy cave into the light of day.

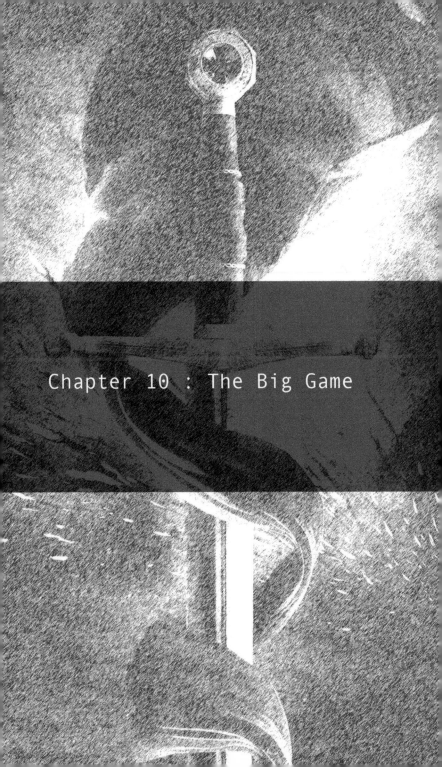

Chapter 10 : The Big Game

The Big Game

"Go suit up," the coach said to Ran. "There are plenty of uniforms your size in the field house.

As Ran jogged happily in to the field house, the team came running out for practice. Ran spotted Gray and tried to get his attention, but Gray looked the other way.

Ten minutes later Ran was given a ball, and he stood on the field while Jude Tripp sat on the bench with a sour expression.

The ball was hiked, and the offensive tackle seemed to work against him, allowing the defense in without a fight. Ran turned on his heels, barely escaping. He hooked around and saw someone open downfield, then launched the ball into orbit, hitting the receiver right in the numbers.

Ran threw the ball with great success for the next few hours of practice. He even noticed the offensive tackle started blocking for him.

Coach blew the whistle, and everyone except Ran and Jude jogged off the field up to the field house to hit the showers.

Ran sat patiently on the hard, white, wooden bench, waiting for coach to tell him if he made the team. Jude held back from showering to talk to Ran.

"Hey," Jude croaked.

"What?" Ran responded defensively, waiting to hear another one of Jude's rude remarks.

"I don't have a computer."

"What?"

"That stupid class where we're in that stupid group . . . I don't have a computer to work on that CD thing."

"Oh." Ran sensed Jude was not being mean, for once. "I don't have a computer, either, but the professor—I mean my grandpa does. I doubt he will let us use it, though. We'll talk to Katie and see if she has one."

"Okay." Jude began to walk off, then turned around, "Hey, you threw pretty well out there today. Coach will probably let you on the team, but don't think you're going to be first string. I've been here longer and the team follows my lead. It takes more than just a good arm to be a quarterback, you know. You've got to be a leader."

"Don't worry, Jude. I don't want to take your spot. I just want a chance to be on the team."

"Whatever. Just do me a favor: Figure out how we're going to get our assignment done."

A few minutes later, Coach walked up to Ran. "You'll play second string in the game against Ashdown on Friday. That means you'll get some playing time."

"What? You're kidding."

"Unless you don't want to."

"No, I can handle it."

"Follow your instincts out there and you'll do fine." Coach sat on the bench and stretched out his legs. "Think your grandfather will come?"

"The professor?" Ran shook his head. "He thinks I'm wasting my time."

"Well, what's important is what you think." Jordan patted Ran's knee. "Now go hit the showers. I'll see you tomorrow."

The week flew by fast. Friday morning came before he knew it. His first game was that evening, and he had practiced hard all week. Jude Tripp ignored him through the week, and Ran barely saw Gray or Katie except in a few classes they had together. The worst class was Mr. Blackhurst's Advanced Life Science. Mr. Blackhurst gave homework every night, and there was to be a test every Monday morning—not to include pop quizzes almost daily. Ran had not passed a quiz yet. So far, he had hidden all his quizzes at school so the professor would not worry. The counselor had signed him up for a tutor, with whom he would meet next Monday after football practice.

Friday's classes were wild. No one listened much because everyone was so excited about the game in Ashdown. At sixth period, while Ran was in Theatre class, an announcement came over the loudspeaker dismissing all football players and cheer leaders. They all met in the basketball gym, and soon the entire school was dismissed to the gym. The band gathered around the team and marched, playing a fight song. The students cheered and Coach Jordan went to the microphone.

"Ladies and gentlemen, boys and girls, we have a new quarterback starting this year for our ninth-grade team. His name is Ran Wisdom. Give him a cheer."

The entire school cheered, and the cheer leaders did back handsprings. Ran gave an embarrassed wave to the crowd.

After the pep rally, the team loaded up on the bus and set course for Ashdown. Ran had brought his CD player and headphones and lay back on his seat, listening to a new praise band from Australia.

When the bus arrived, the team's center, Danny Cook, had to wake Ran. He had fallen asleep and was drooling on his hand.

"What?"

"Dude, we're here. Get up before coach sees you sleeping."

Ran jumped up and started to walk off the bus when he realized his shoes were very slippery. When he started to fall, he reached for the seats beside him, but missed. His feet went out from under him, and he landed on his back.

"What happened?" Coach Jordan yelled as he rushed to the back of the bus from the driver's seat, but it was too late. Ran had bruised his tailbone.

"Let's get the paramedic in here to look at you." Jordan said.

"Coach, it's my shoes—they're real slippery."

Coach Jordan examined Ran's shoes. "Someone put baby oil on your shoes, boy." Coach got up and turned around, yelling, "If I find out who did this, they will never play on this team again." He cursed and stomped off the bus.

Ran did not have to think long for a suspect: Jude Tripp.

The paramedics took Ran to St. Michael's Emergency Room, where he was x-rayed. Flipping his chart, the doctor looked at Ran and said, "All I can give you is pain medicine. You have a bruised tailbone and will have to rest from football for at least two weeks."

"Doc, can't I play next week?" Ran asked, as the doctor wrote a prescription and handed him some samples.

"Son, you won't be able to play for about two weeks, at the least." The doctor showed Ran to the door, and Ran limped back to the waiting room.

Two hours later, the team came rushing into the hospital waiting area, where Ran, under the influence of pain medication, sat on a pillow. He was feeling pretty good by the time the team arrived.

"We won!" Danny grinned as he handed Ran the winning football. "We all signed the ball for you. You're the first person on the team who has ever been injured before they got to play a game."

Gray pulled Ran aside when everyone was loading the

bus. "Have a nice trip? See ya next fall. Ha, ha, hee, hee."

"What?" Ran asked, but Gray jumped onto the bus, laughing hysterically.

On the ride home, Ran sang really loud every song he could think of for the team. They laughed as he even tried to dance, but his backside kept hurting every time he stood.

"Next week I'm bringing my guitar. If I can't throw the football for two weeks, I will be our entertainment."

Coach Jordan looked at him through the rearview mirror with a grin and said, "You'll be back quicker than that. I have some techniques that will have you back in shape in a week. And it does not include that medicine, which is making your singing sound like a sick mule." The bus erupted in laughter.

"But Coach Jordan, why do you need me back? You guys won without me."

Everyone on the bus went silent. Ran was asking a private question in public.

"Never mind. You'd better go back to singing before you get yourself in deeper."

Ran didn't dare go back to sleep, and everyone was tired of hearing him sing, so he decided to read his Life Science book. The bus arrived back late, and Granny Wisdom was waiting to pick Ran up. Before Ran could get to the car, Jude stopped him. Granny saw them talking and got out of the Cadillac.

"You need some help with your things, Ran?" Granny asked, concerned for Ran. He had told her about some of the boys being rude to him.

"No, Grandma, I'm fine," Ran answered.

Jude whispered, "Everyone thinks I had something to do with you falling, but I didn't. I would never go that far. Look, I know who did it."

"Who?"

"Gray Floyd."

Ran thought he was imagining things. "What?"

"Hey, dude, you didn't hear it from me, but maybe it's because Katie broke up with him last Monday." Jude tossed his gym bag over his shoulder. "Hey, remember tomorrow afternoon we're meeting to work on World Cultures. Did you get to talk to Katie about a computer?"

"No. I guess I forgot." Ran saw Granny waiting. "Look, just come over to my house, and we will figure something out. I've got to go."

Chapter 11 :
Through the Looking Glass

Through the Looking Glass

Before Ran fell asleep, he thought about what Jude had said. Did Gray really cause his accident? Why didn't Katie tell him she was going out with Gray? Why did she break up with Gray? Before his mind found any answers, the medicine did its work, putting Ran to sleep.

The next morning his tailbone was in agony, so he took another pill and slept in until noon. Granny Wisdom brought lunch to him in bed, and every once in a while he opened his Life Science book.

By one o'clock he was up, showered, and cleaning his room. He was expecting his guests at two, and Granny Wisdom was going to the church for a women's quilting bee. The professor decided to drop her off at the side door—it was as close as he would get to going to church—and then hie himself off to the library to do some research.

The house was empty, and the old grandfather clock was ticking loudly in the quiet living room. Ran ate ice cream as he waited. Finally the doorbell rang, and Ran could see Katie and her mother outside through the windows. Ran opened the door and, as he stepped outside, noticed that a storm was approaching on the horizon.

"Hi, Ran. This is my mom, Betty," Katie said.

"Hi, Mrs. Summers. Nice to meet you." Ran made an effort to fix his hair before shaking her hand.

"Is your grandmother home?"

"No, she's working on a quilting project with the ladies at church—and Grandpa's gone to the library."

"Oh, yes, I forgot. They've been inviting me to come, but you know how busy things get. Well, I guess I can trust you with my daughter alone, being you're a preacher's kid—I mean used to be—I mean . . ." Mrs. Summers blushed.

"It's okay, Mrs. Summers. You could still say I'm a preacher's kid."

"Well, I'll be back at 6:00 to pick up Katie. Be good, darling. Y'all be careful, there's a bad storm brewing. Don't go outside in it." She kissed Katie on the cheek, and Ran sensed it embarrassed Katie.

"All right, Mom, 'bye." Katie's mother got into her sports utility vehicle and drove away.

"I am so sorry about my mom. She is a freak."

"I didn't think so." Ran opened the door and watched her go in. She was wearing blue jeans and a tank top. Her perfume lingered behind her.

Ran could not believe she was at his house and they were alone.

No wonder Gray's out to kill me, Ran thought, as they sat down.

"Can I get you something to drink—some ice cream—anything?"

"No, I'm fine. How's your—uh—you know?"

"My butt." They laughed. "It's fine. Doctor says I'll be good as new in a few weeks. Good thing, too, because I didn't want to get it amputated."

Katie laughed so hard she snorted. "Oops. I'm sorry. I just can't help it. When I get around you, I never know what I'm going to do."

KNOCK, KNOCK, KNOCK!

"That must be Jude." Ran opened the door and stood aside quickly when Jude hurried in, raindrops scattering everywhere as he shook himself like a wet puppy.

"Hey, it's raining like crazy out there. Here, I brought this." Jude pulled chips out of his paper bag, and underneath was a six-pack of beer. "I swiped it from our refrigerator. It's my dad's."

"You shouldn't have," Ran said, as he took the bag and placed it on the counter.

"No problem." Jude went and sat next to Katie. "How you doing?"

"No, Jude, you really shouldn't have. We are studying this afternoon, and besides, if my grandparents find out there was beer in their house, I will be grounded for a lifetime, which means no more studying at my house." Ran took the six-pack and tossed it in the garbage can.

"Oh, sorry, dude. I was just trying to bring a gift."

"Well, thank you." Ran realized that Jude really did not know better.

Suddenly thunder boomed outside. The rain began pounding the roof of his grandparents' house.

As she moved away from Jude on the couch, Katie asked, "Where are we studying, anyway?"

"In my room." They made their way to the study, and Ran found three chairs to put around the computer. He pulled out the CD-ROM textbook and inserted it into the drive.

Katie was shocked. "Do you think the professor will mind if you use his computer?"

Ran looked guilty. "Well, he said I couldn't use it, but what are we supposed to do? Besides, they'll be gone for a few hours."

"It doesn't sound like the Christian thing to do, Ran," Jude croaked.

An angel appeared on the screen. "Hello, and welcome to Old Testament Survey: Four Adventures through Time. I am Theta, your guide for the journey. If you have a question, just click the Help icon and I will be there to help you with explanations or maps."

At this time, the angel flew dramatically around the

screen, and then the screen showed a bird's-eye view of a large, green forest, and Ran could see several animals roaming around like tiny ants far below. It was like being in an airplane and looking out the window, but better. He had never seen such a beautiful landscape. The angel flew through the clouds and hovered in the air. "You have been chosen."

The angel pulled out a trumpet and blew it dramatically. "Without your help, the truth of God's word will be lost to your generation. You are special to the heart of God and part of His plan. God desires for you to know Him as He desires to know you."

Jude yawned. "Ugh. What is this about? Can you press a button and skip this part?"

The angel continued. "On this particular adventure through time, you will be placed in the Garden of Eden. Your objective is to answer these questions. Who is the God of the Bible? Who is Man? Was there a Garden of Eden or a Garden IN Eden? Why did Adam and Eve choose their will over God's will?

Lastly, where is the Garden now?"

KABOOM!

Lightning flashed outside Ran's house, the power went out, and sparks flew from the back of the computer.

Katie screamed.

"Are you all right?" Ran asked, as they all groped around in the dark. Katie found Ran and held onto him.

"I'm okay," croaked Jude.

Katie and Ran laughed. "I meant is Katie all right," Ran said.

"Oh," Jude chuckled.

The lights came back on, and Jude looked at them hugging. "Uh, I guess I better not say anything to Gray about this?"

"I just grabbed onto him because I was scared." Katie blushed. They let go of each other quickly. "Oh, my gosh, look at the computer."

At first Ran thought Katie was trying to change the subject, but on second glance, Ran noticed that the computer screen was swirling with an array of colors.

"Oh, no! My grandfather is going to kill me."

Jude reached out his hand toward the computer.

Katie grabbed his hand. "Wait—what if it electrocutes you?"

Jude moved toward the screen, "I don't think that's going to happen."

Before anyone could stop him, Jude touched the screen. A light flashed through the room again, but this time a bright, white light came from the computer screen and a voice, "Welcome to Eden, Jude Tripp."

Katie and Ran watched Jude's hand disappear into the computer screen. Jude looked back at Ran. "What—"

Then something happened that neither Ran nor Jude nor Katie could understand. Suddenly Jude disappeared. A bright, white light flashed from the computer screen.

Ran was speechless.

"Where did he go, Ran?" Katie cried.

"Everything's going to be all right. There has to be a logical answer to this."

Ran picked up the phone to dial 911. "The phone's dead. Katie—"

Katie was silent, her hands over her mouth.

"—I think I'm going to have to go in there and get him out."

"Go into where? Where did he go?"

"I'm not sure, but maybe if I touch the screen, I'll find

out," Ran said. "I have no choice."

"No way, Ran. We have no way of knowing what happened to him. He might be dead. I am not going to let that happen to you. I just met you, and . . . I just don't want to see you get hurt."

"Katie, I have to go. I can't just sit here. He may be on the other side, waiting for someone to help him."

"On the other side of what? You are talking crazy!"

"Maybe so, but I'm going to touch this screen and find out. I have no choice."

"Fine, but I'm going to touch it, too. If you go somewhere, I'm not staying here alone."

"No, you're not going, too! You are going to stay here until my grandparents come home, and, if I don't come back, you can tell them what happened to us."

"I'm sorry, but I will not stay here in this house alone." Ran had never seen Katie angry. Her cheeks were bright pink and her eyes were wide open.

"All right. On the count of three, we will touch the screen together." Ran took her hand. "One, two, three—" they touched and the bright light pierced the room again.

They heard someone talking. "Welcome to Eden, Katie Summers and Ran Wisdom." They felt their feet leave the ground, and like soda through a straw, they were sucked into another dimension.

For several seconds, they floated through what looked like wet paint of all colors swirling around them.

Then they were floating through space at rocket speed. They saw Earth below them and felt themselves falling rapidly.

The ground rushed up under their feet. No parachute was available.

"Ran, we're falling!" Katie screamed.

"We'll be okay," Ran assured her.

"How?"

"Because we're going to land in that laaaaake!"

SPLOOSH!

Katie swam to the shore. "Where are we, Ran?"

"You are in Eden." The voice came from somewhere up in the forest. They searched with their eyes to see who was speaking.

Katie screamed again, this time for good reason. They were looking up the hillside at a large lion.

The lion slowly sauntered down the hill. "You look as shocked as the other guy who just came through here, although he did not stay to chat. He ran the other way."

"Uh . . . um." Ran was petrified.

"Can either of you speak?" The lion waited for a few moments.

Katie screamed again.

"My, you have a very loud way of saying hello."

Ran gathered his thoughts. Why was there a talking lion? Where had he seen a talking lion before—where? Oh, yes, there was a talking lion in the C.S. Lewis book, but why was there a talking lion on the other side of his computer screen? Where was he? Ran paused to look around at the forest. The trees were bright green, and every tree bore fruit—banana trees, apple trees, orange trees, peach trees, and many other fruits Ran had never seen.

From where he stood he could see that this was like a tropical forest. As he looked down into the valley it was like there was a garden inside this beautiful, tropical paradise.

Then he got it. He was in the Garden of Eden. He was in the computer program. This was all part of the CD-ROM textbook.

"Well, if you're not going to talk to me, I'll be leaving."

The lion turned around.

"No, wait. It just took me a moment to figure out where I was," Ran said. Katie looked at him. "I know I must seem to be acting strange—yes, indeed. It's just that we've never spoken with an animal before."

"Quite a shame. Adam and I talk every day—especially since he named me Lion and appointed me King of Beasts—a silly title, really. I am not actually the king. You see, Adam is over me, and we all know who is the real King, don't we?" Lion gestured toward the sky, but in the direction of the more beautiful part. The part that seemed to be a perfect garden.

Katie held onto Ran. "Where are we, and what is that animal doing talking to us?"

"Oh, I should have explained when I figured it out," Ran said. "Katie, this is the Garden of Eden, and this lion here is one of the animals in the Garden."

"How did we get in the Garden of Eden, Ran?" Katie asked and tried to smile at Lion.

"I'm not exactly sure. All I can figure is that somehow we got inside the computer textbook," Ran said.

"But books aren't in three dimensions now, are they?" Katie squeezed Ran's arm tighter.

"Ouch. I don't know."

"Ran, one more question." Katie managed another fake smile and whispered, "How come that lion is talking?"

"I don't know. Why don't you stop squeezing my arm and ask him?"

Katie managed to give her biggest grin. "Excuse me, Mr. Lion, sir, I have one question: How is it you can talk?"

"That's easy. All the animals in Eden can talk, and some talk too much, if you ask me—especially the reptiles. They're very opinionated. They think they should have been appointed king. But Adam said he needs a leader with a level head, and that is where I come into the picture."

Ran was thinking about the story of Adam and Eve. He had not read Genesis in a while. "Katie, do you remember how the snake talks to Eve in the book of Genesis?"

"Sure," Katie said. She finally let go of Ran's arm.

"Maybe—whatever kind of interactive textbook we've gotten into here, by accident or purpose—maybe the writers of the program assumed all animals could talk."

"I have no idea what you two are talking about, and I don't mean to be rude, but shouldn't you be going to look for your friend?" asked Lion.

"You're right," Ran agreed. "Do you know where he is? We really need to find him and be leaving."

"Leave Eden? Hmm, I have never heard of such a thing. No. In fact, I do not know why you would want to leave. Everything we need is here: fresh fruit, plenty of water, good friends. Speaking of friends, I am not sure where your friend headed off to in such a hurry."

Katie reached over and picked fruit from a tree and started to taste it. "I'll bet even the fruit tastes good," she said.

Lion quickly objected, "I wouldn't do that if I were you. Adam says humans are never to eat from that tree. It has the knowledge of good and evil in it. I'm not sure what that is, but I follow the orders of Adam."

Looking at the forbidden fruit and the tree of ancient mystery, Katie was perplexed. "This is what caused all the problems, huh? It doesn't look like much. I thought there would be some dramatic light shining down on this tree or something, but it's just a tree and this fruit just looks like regular fruit."

Katie poked Ran. "This is too wild. Well, if we got here through the computer, how do we get out?"

"I don't know. I wish that angel, Theslo or whatever, was here to help us out." Ran answered.

"You mean Theta?" Katie asked.

Just then, from out of the sky, flying like a dove from heaven, I, Theta, came and landed next to Lion.

"Hello, Ran and Katie," I said. "I am Theta, your guide. Can I help you?"

They were baffled when I appeared.

"Wow!" Ran stammered, amazed. "Yes. We need to find our friend and leave the program."

"I can help you find your friend, but I am afraid that leaving right now is impossible."

"What?"

"I am sorry, but you may not leave until you are ready to answer the questions."

"How long will that last?" Ran asked.

"I am not sure," I said.

"Some help you are." Ran walked away, kicking the bushes around him.

Katie tried to help by asking, "Theta, could you tell us where our friend is and what we are supposed to do in this adventure?"

I was proud of Katie for keeping her cool. "Yes. First, your friend is one mile north, hiding in a cave. Here is a map." Walking toward Katie, I handed her a map. "Second, you are not here to do anything. You are here to gain a revelation. A revelation of who God is and who you are."

Ran was overwhelmed. "I already know all that stuff."

Calmly I replied, "You think you do. Even if you did,

you have not shared it with your friends. Submit to the adventure, then all will be well."

With these words, I stretched out my wings and shot like lightning through the sky.

Ran grabbed the map from Katie's hand and said through his teeth, "Great. Let's go find Jude. If we are gone too long, our folks are going to wonder what has happened."

Almost a mile north, Ran turned around and noticed Katie lagging behind. "Come on, Katie. I think the cave is right over the next hill."

"I'm coming." Katie gasped for air.

"Well, not fast enough. We've got to find Jude so we can get out of this computer program." Ran trudged up the hill.

When Katie finally caught up to him, she asked, "Are you sweating?"

"What?"

"I'm sweating something awful," she said.

"Well, I'm sorry, but we've been walking pretty fast." Ran was growing breathless as they reached the top of the hill.

Katie looked at him. "And you're breathing hard, too."

"What's your point?" Ran asked.

"If this is just a computer program, why are we sweating and breathing hard, and why does everything look so real?"

Ran turned and looked at Katie, puzzled. "We don't have time for twenty questions, Katie. We've got to find Jude and get out of here."

Katie looked up at the cave only yards in front of them.

"Ran, I don't think we are in a computer program."

"Where do you think we are?" Ran asked, as he stopped to catch his breath.

Katie looked down, thinking. "I'm not sure, but I think we really are in the Garden of Eden."

"That's impossible. The Garden of Eden was closed six thousand years ago, when Adam and Eve ate the forbidden fruit. God set Cherubims and a flaming sword to guard the entrance."

Katie looked at Ran with a serious look. "Maybe something really odd happened when the lightning hit the computer—I don't know, maybe when we touched the screen, we went back in time."

"Ha! Very unlikely," Ran said.

"Why not? Look around you. Everything looks real. It doesn't look like any graphics I've ever seen on a computer game. Have you looked at the sky? It is covered in a hazy fog. Pastor Preacher said that creation scientists believe Eden was covered by a protective . . ."

Ran cut her off before she finished, "Yes, a protective canopy of fog that gave Eden a greenhouse effect. The writers of the program thought of this and simply added the visual effect to the program."

"Forget it. Let's go find Jude." Katie marched into the cave, leaving Ran puzzled about what he had said that was so offensive.

When Ran went into the cave, the entrance was low and he had to crouch to enter. "Katie, I'm sorry." He looked down a dark narrow pathway. He did not see her. He yelled, "Katie, come back here. I am probably wrong. Maybe we did go back in time." He did not believe he was wrong, but thought she would like to hear him say it.

Ran heard something stir down the path. "Katie, is

that you?" He hurried to the end of the narrow corridor, which opened into a larger cave room. He stood at the top of a cavern and peered down into the cave, which was shaped like a bowl, and, looking down, he could see several different types of reptiles gathering around two figures. Even as he descended down into the cavern, he recognized who they were.

Jude and Katie were surrounded by the reptiles, and one of the reptiles seemed to be the leader of the pack—a Komodo dragon, who weighed around 2500 pounds! The reptile paced around the two of them, slowly swinging his tail behind him like a ticking clock.

His wild, red eyes bulged as he questioned Jude with a hiss, "I will ask you one more time: Where did you come from?"

Katie looked at Jude to see what he would say. A few tense moments passed. The Komodo dragon then raised his body up and stood on his hind legs, ready to attack. "You are not the chosen one—Adam." He pointed a sharp claw at Jude's throat. "We don't welcome strangers here."

Just then a small lizard spied Ran at the top of the cavern and yelled, "There's another one up there. Let's get him."

Ran looked around for a weapon as the reptiles approached him. He looked up and saw a stalactite hanging from the cave ceiling. Jumping up, he knocked it loose. Suddenly a long-nosed alligator snapped at his ankles.

Ran jumped back and forced the stalactite down toward the animal, driving it directly into the alligator's right eye. Blood squirted everywhere and covered Gator's face. Shocked, the reptiles backed away.

The Komodo dragon examined the beast. "What did you do to Gator?"

"He tried to bite me, so I . . ."

Ran started to walk toward the beast, feeling sorry. Just as he did, the reptiles turned on him to attack.

Ran darted for the top of the cave, jumping over a blue-and-yellow lizard. The other reptiles advanced quickly. A large tail swept Ran off his feet. He hit the stone floor of the cave with a thud. Blood seeped down his face as he tumbled toward the cavern embankment. He looked up to see at least thirty pointed snouts and yellow, angled eyes staring at him, all wanting revenge.

Ran closed his eyes, and a thought came to his mind.

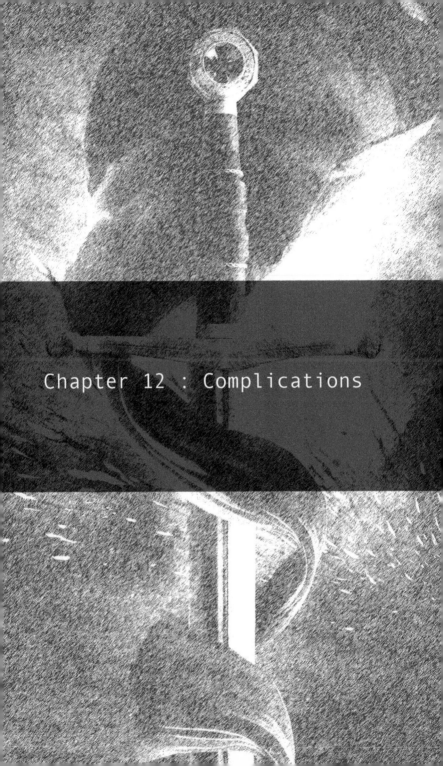

Chapter 12 : Complications

Complications

The Wisdoms' house was quiet and peaceful. The sounds of rain now replaced by birds chirping, the smell that comes after a hard rain, and the heavy weight of humidity lingered in the air. All seemed calm, but trouble was near. Gray Floyd stood outside the Wisdoms' home, and beside him was his sidekick Vance. Gray had rung the doorbell twice, but no one answered.

"I know they're in there," Gray said to his buddy Vance.

"Nah, let's go. Let's go eat pizza," Vance said.

"No! I know he's in there with my girlfriend, and I am not going to let him get away with it."

"I thought you and Ran used to be friends."

Gray laughed. "Used to be, before he came back here to ruin everything."

"What do you mean?"

"Let's see," Gray talked as he walked the back of the house, spying in each window. "He took my girlfriend and my spot on the football team."

"What? You're the receiver," Vance argued.

"That's what I am talking about. How did he know I wanted to try out for quarterback? He knew and came back to ruin me."

"That's crazy, Gray. His father died."

"Shh! Look in the window there. See that computer? That's where they're supposed to be working. I knew it. He took her out on a date."

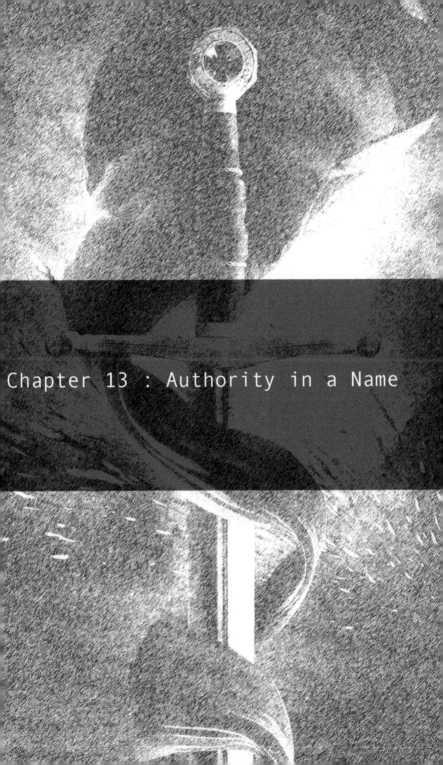

Chapter 13 : Authority in a Name

Authority in a Name

Ran managed to put his thoughts together. All the years of Bible training flashed through his mind. He knew what he should do.

The reptiles were poised to strike him, but before they could make their move, Ran said with authority, "As a son of Adam, I command you to get out of here and never bother us again."

The reptiles seemed confused. They looked at each other and talked in whispers in a foreign tongue. Then, silently, they cowered and walked, one by one, away from him. Eventually each one left the cave.

Running toward Ran, Katie squealed with joy, "How did you know what to say?"

"I'm not sure. I just figured they had to answer to authority. Kind of like demons: If you use the name of Jesus, they must flee." Ran got up and dusted off his clothes and put his hand on his head.

Jude approached him, saying, "If they belong to Adam and this is the perfect Garden of Eden, then why did they try to attack you? I thought Eden was supposed to be perfect."

"Because there is a great division in the animal kingdom," a voice spoke from behind them. Startled, they turned to find Lion standing only a few yards away.

"I see you have met the reptiles. Since the day I met Adam and he named me, he told me to watch out for all reptiles. I believe they are up to something, but I have yet to figure out exactly what it is. . ."

Ran was confused. "I don't understand. How can there be division in the animal kingdom?"

Lion walked slowly down into the cave. "I'm not really

sure, but I think that is why Adam appointed me King of Beasts. Adam believes we are not alone in Eden—that is, he thinks there is more here than animals and humans."

Katie spoke up. "Who else could there be?"

"I don't know, but I think something very evil," Lion answered.

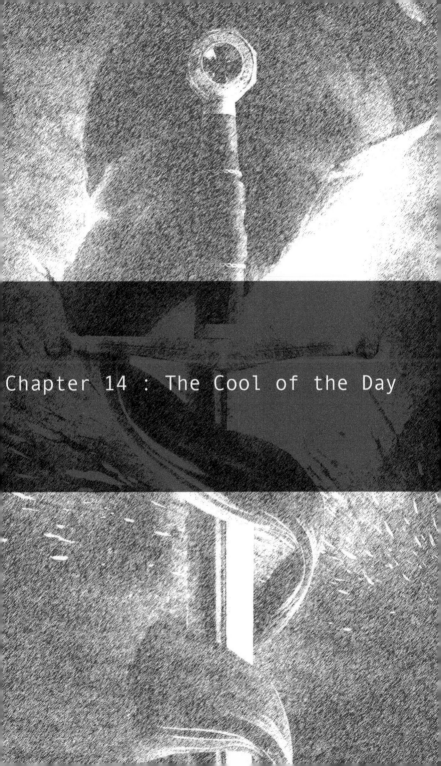

Chapter 14 : The Cool of the Day

The Cool of the Day

Three miles away in a marsh valley, Adam and Eve walked in the cool of the day with their Creator. At the same time, Ran, Jude and Katie were following Lion up a mountain trail. When they reached the peak, they rested. They were all hungry, so Katie picked a few peaches while Ran gathered berries. After they ate, Jude slept under a large oak tree and Lion grazed on grass. Ran and Katie sat looking over the valley. A lark sang his song in a nearby tree.

Talking to Katie, Ran looked back and motioned toward Lion, "Did you know that in the Garden of Eden animals did not eat each other? Everyone was a vegetarian."

"Yes. I remember Pastor Preacher saying that even dinosaurs lived off the land. Mr. Blackhurst wouldn't agree in Earth Science class. He thinks Creation Science is a joke. I heard that one student challenged him in front of the class, and, on his next test, he gave an essay question asking how the earth was formed."

"What happened?"

"The student wrote a six-page essay, citing proofs of a six-day creation. Blackhurst turned the papers back the next week. He gave her an F. Her parents even came up to the school, but he wouldn't budge. He gave her a choice. She could take the F or she could write a new essay on evolution."

Ran sat up as he asked, "So what did she do?"

"She wrote the paper. She was our valedictorian last year." Katie leaned back on the ground and breathed in a deep breath.

"Katie, what do you think about Pastor Preacher?" Ran had been waiting for someone to talk to about him.

"He's. . . okay. I don't know. I guess he means well, why?"

Ran sighed, "I don't know. I get a strange vibe. Not sure, sometimes people make bad first impressions."

Katie chuckled, "You referring to you or him?"

"What's that supposed to mean?" He reached over and grabbed a peach and threw it at her. In fun, of course, but hard enough to bounce off the side of her head and cause her to bust out laughing. Next thing you know, she tackled Ran and the two were wrestling. They both finally, fell onto their backs staring into the most beautiful colorful sky they ever laid eyes on.

It was this moment they both realized how great they felt. They both felt better than they ever had in their entire lives. Ran was sure there was no drug on earth that could compare to the feeling of being in this place. Their was a presence of joy bursting from every blade of grass and he even thought the fruit from the trees were talking to him.

They were in the garden part of Eden. Just then he realized this was a garden in Eden not a garden of Eden. They had wondered into something amazing.

"Gosh, even the air is better here. I'm starting to feel like I never want to leave," Ran exclaimed.

He rolled over on his stomach next to Katie and sat up on his elbows, looking into her blue eyes. "Can you believe anyone would ever want to leave this?"

Just then Lion jumped up, startled. "Someone's coming!"

Up the trail three horses galloped. The one in the lead was a black stallion with a long flowing mane. "Hail, Lion, King of Beasts. We come with news from the east."

Lion's ears perked. "What is it?"

The second horse, a speckled Appaloosa, stepped

forward. "The reptiles are very angry, sir. One of their own was wounded and has lost his eye. They are planning revenge."

Lion turned his head and glanced at Ran and then turned back toward the horses. "What do they plan?"

The speckled horse shook his head, "They are talking to the dinosaurs."

Within Eden, animals heard of other animals that lived outside the tangled forest. The animals were thought to be long extinct before Man was created. They were from a time when darkness covered the earth. To hear that the reptiles were in contact with them or that they were coming into Eden from outside it's borders was the most dire news Lion could have been given. The worst part is that the myths of some of these creatures were more frightful than others, so the first question arising in Lion's mind was of course:

"Which ones?"

"Not just one group. They met with T-Rex and the Pterodactyls. An alliance is forming now." The speckled horse bowed his head and stepped back.

"Hmm. Not good. Not good at all. We need to get them to safety quickly." Lion paced back and forth in deep thought.

The third horse, a dark brown Clydesdale, stepped forward. We can help, my king."

"What's your plan, Clydesdale?" Lion asked.

"Your guests, my master, can ride on our backs." Clydesdale jerked his head, motioning toward Ran, Katie and Jude.

Lion raised his brow. "Humph. Never heard of that."

"Adam has ridden on our backs before. He seems to enjoy it, sir. Anyhow, we can get them to safety quicker than they can run."

"True. I need to tell Adam and Eve what has happened," Lion said in a weary voice.

Katie stepped forward toward Lion. "I don't think that's a good idea. I don't think Adam should know we are here."

Lion laughed. "Sorry, Katie, but Adam and Eve are to know everything that goes on in this Garden, and it's my job to inform them."

Katie argued, "But we're not supposed to be here, Lion. You don't know this now, but one day someone's going to write a story about this place. If we get involved in the story, everything will change."

The black horse interrupted the argument. "Excuse me. I do not mean to be rude, but, as we speak, trouble brews. Let us take the three to the cave where the water falls. Behind the water is a cavern. They can find shelter there. Night approaches soon."

Ran was angry. "We cannot spend the night. I have got to get back to my grandparents, and my friends have parents who are going to be worried."

Lion turned his head and looked at Ran through his thick mane. "Young Ran, I know you must leave soon, but neither one of us knows how to get you home. Even Theta said you must stay until your mission is complete. Go with Clydesdale, Stallion and Appaloosa. They will keep you safe until we can figure something out."

After Lion spoke, Katie, Ran and Jude got on the backs of the great beasts, and off they galloped toward safety. The sky was pink, and night grew near.

Chapter 15 : A Snag in Paradise

A Snag in Paradise

"Masters Adam and Eve, I do not mean to disturb you as you meet with the Almighty Creator." Lion bowed before Adam and Eve. They turned and looked at him.

The Almighty God also turned around. "Lion, good to see you." Beams of light burst from His face as He smiled.

"Blessing, glory and honor to Your kingdom forever, my Lord and True Master," Lion said, as he bowed his head even further to the ground. An excitement ran through his soul as he praised the Almighty God. "I praise Thee with my whole heart."

"Arise, Lion." The Almighty God walked toward him. His skin was bronze, His eyes were as fire, and His hair was as wool. His feet were as brass, and to stand in His presence was too glorious to explain. He placed His hand on Lion's mane and stroked him between the ears. "Adam tells me he has appointed you King of the Beasts. You will serve him well." He reached down and embraced Lion and kissed his cheek. "I must return to My Father now." He turned back to Adam and Eve. "Peace, my brother and sister."

Lion looked at Adam and The Almighty. The resemblance between the two was uncanny. They looked like brothers, except The Almighty's glory shone forth much brighter. The Almighty One hugged Adam and Eve, kissing them on the cheek. He then ascended into the sky beyond the haze and eventually out of sight.

Adam looked at Lion. "What is the urgency, good friend?"

"There is trouble stirring in the animal kingdom, sir," Lion said.

"What do you mean?" Adam knelt down, making his face even with Lion's, and Eve stood behind him.

"One of the reptiles has been injured. He lost his eye in a battle."

"Did you gather fruit from the Tree of Health? All he has to do is eat the fruit and he will be made whole." Adam stood and walked to a nearby tree. He picked three pieces of fruit, and, offering them to Lion then, he said, "Here, take this quickly to him."

"Sir, the reptiles do not seem to want to take time for healing. They seek revenge. They have even formed an alliance with T-Rex and Pterodactyl." Lion could sense that Adam was not happy.

Adam dropped the fruit and kicked a nearby bush. "Who caused this injury? No one in my kingdom will inflict pain." Adam knelt again and spoke to Lion in a whisper, "I hear word there is an ancient spirit who walks the forest at night while we sleep. Have you heard tell of such a one?"

Lion bowed his head. "Yes, sir, I have." Looking back up, he said, "Sir, the one who caused this injury is not the ancient one you speak of, but I do believe his evil is behind this. The reptile Gator was the one who provoked the fight, sir. I was there. He attacked the one who inflicted the wound."

"Lion, why do you talk to me in riddles? Tell me plainly: Who caused this injury?"

Lion had no choice; he must tell his master. "Sir, there are three strangers from outside of Eden. One of them caused the injury."

Adam stood up. "From outside of Eden? I have never heard of such a thing. What kind of animals are they?"

"Sir, they are not animal. They are like you." Lion was not sure how Adam would react.

A few silent moments passed. Adam finally spoke,

"Lion, I need you to tell me where they stay."

"Sir, with all due respect, I do not think you should meet them. Besides, they said they are leaving soon. I'm not even sure they will be there when you arrive."

Adam spoke in an understanding voice, "My thoughts are not your thoughts. Tell me where they shelter for the night."

"They stay behind the water that falls, my lord," Lion said.

Adam grabbed Eve's hands. "I am going to investigate, my love. Please gather us something to eat. I will be back shortly." Adam kissed Eve. He then turned to Lion. "Are my horses near?"

"They are with the humans, sir." Lion answered.

"Then we shall run." With these words, Adam and Lion started toward the waterfalls.

At the same time, on the opposite side of Eden, the horses reached the falls. Ran, Katie and Jude dismounted and followed the horses up a path of sharp, angled rocks. Behind the falls was a narrow hole in the side of the mountain, where they squeezed through to find an open space. After they were in the cave, they stood behind the waterfall, amazed at its power. The rushing water was very loud. It produced a cool mist.

Clydesdale raised his voice loudly to be heard, "We must leave you now." He tossed his head and pointed his nose to show them a direction. "Over there is a path that will lead you deeper into this cave. There you will find a place to rest. You should be safe from danger now. We will be nearby, watching, in case trouble arrives. We will send a warning if it does." He bowed his head. Stallion and Appaloosa followed him out of the cave.

Jude put his hand under the falls to taste the water. "Very refreshing. I've been so thirsty."

Ran and Katie also drank from the falls. After quenching their thirst, they walked up the path into a larger room and laid down to rest. Katie looked at Ran. "How long do you think we have been here?"

Ran looked at his watch. It was blank. "Hmm. My watch isn't working. It must have malfunctioned when we traveled through the portal."

Jude sat up. "I would say we've been here about five hours."

Ran sighed and laid back. "Great. That means our folks are looking for us right now."

"I'm the one to blame for this. I shouldn't have touched the screen in the first place." Jude said.

Katie reached over and touched Jude's arm. "Don't blame yourself, Jude. You had no idea all of this would happen."

Jude stood and dusted off his clothes. "I can't sleep." He paced around in a circle. "I don't think we're going to get out of here any sooner by hiding out in this cave."

Ran tossed a pebble against the wall. "So what do you propose we do—go out and fight T-Rex, Pterodactyl and Alligator? Who knows how many other animals they have found to help them." He tossed another pebble. "This is all my fault."

Katie was sitting by Ran. She placed her hand on his arm. "It's not your fault, either, Ran. You had no choice. You were defending yourself." She leaned her head against Ran's shoulder. "I'm starting to get worried. What if we never make it out of here?"

"I don't know. Theta said we would."

"Oh, yeah, where is he?"

Just then I, Theta, flew into the cave and stood beside Katie. I stared at the three. "Did you need me?"

Katie was excited to see me. "Yes. We don't know what to do. Ran got into a fight with Alligator, and now he is coming after us for revenge."

Ran added, "He's also got T-Rex and Pterodactyl with him."

I presently flapped my wings and hovered above them. "Yes, you seem to be in a little trouble."

Ran's temper topped again, "A LITTLE TROUBLE?" He leaped to his feet. "We have been here all day. We are hungry, tired and ready to go home."

Of course I knew none of this was true, but I let him continue.

"Our folks are probably worrying themselves to death."

"Randall Wisdom, Jr., sit down." My voice was a force of authority that caused Ran to sit quickly. "Don't worry about your folks. Have you not figured out yet that you are not here by accident? I did not bring you here to learn a few facts and write a paper." I sat on a nearby boulder.

"Not here by accident? Do you mean you caused the thunderstorm that electrocuted my computer? You set all this up?"

I nodded.

"While we're on that subject, why did you bring us here?" Ran interjected.

"I told you when you first turned the program on: You three have been chosen. You are a holy priesthood and a chosen generation. All of those chosen before you rarely met their assigned angel; they were led by thoughts and circumstances. However, you are a special generation before Christ's return to Earth, so it is important that you come to know who God is and who you are."

They gazed puzzled at these words. I tried a different tactic.

"Ran, is it true that you still think you are in a computer program?"

Ran fumbled for words.

Katie looked at Ran. "I told you we were really here."

"Yes." I explained: "You are here, but it's like a vision. There is a prophecy in the book of Joel and also repeated in the book of Acts. It says that young men shall see visions and old men shall dream dreams. You are having a vision. The Apostle Paul and the Apostle John both had them. You have been chosen to see this place and many others before it is all over."

Ran asked, "Before what is all over?"

"All three of you will be visiting me this year three more times, and three more times next semester of school. Before it is over, I have made plans for us to have many adventures. You are to focus on learning as much as you can about the Old Testament. At the beginning of your next semester, you will visit me again to learn about the New Testament. Before the school year ends, you will have visited quite a few places, and you will meet many of those great men and women who went before you."

"There is only one thing I don't understand, Theta." Ran said.

"What?"

"Why me? Why us?"

I chose my words, "Why not?"

Ran leaned his head forward into his hands. He ran his fingers through his hair. "I'm sorry. This whole thing is just a little too hard to believe. We're all ready to go home. Just tell us what we're supposed to do."

I answered in a kind, calm tone, "Wait 'til morning. Everything will seem much clearer then." With these words, I spread out my wings and left the cave in a flash.

The three teens sat quietly for a moment, staring at each other. Katie spoke first. "Ran, I hate to say I told you so, but—"

"Yeah, I hear you. I still don't understand Theta. He's supposed to be our guide, but he never tells us anything helpful." Ran took another handful of pebbles and began tossing.

"Ran, why—" Katie started to say something but stopped herself.

Ran looked up at her and sighed, "What?"

"Nothing." She could not help herself. "Ran, why are you always so angry? I mean, I know you've had some hard times, but so have the rest of us. I just mean, when you were at church on Sunday, you got up on the stage, and you sounded like a totally different person. Look, dude, you just got told the most awesome news any person on Earth would be falling to their knees and thanking God to hear. You have been chosen, by God, for a special purpose, and God wants to use you for something special.

"That's just it. God wants to USE ME!!! Just like he

USED MY MOTHER. Just like He USED MY FATHER!!!"

Fireworks burst inside Ran's brain. He started to hyperventilate.

Jude came to his side and croaked, "Just sit down, dude. It's okay. Just breathe."

A few moments passed. The three sat together, Ran in the middle. Katie and Jude knew how awful it must be to lose both parents.

Ran did not normally like people getting into his personal business, but for the first time in a long time, he felt truly loved by these two new friends.

After a while Jude went over and sat across the room. A cold chill crept across his back. Little did he know how close he was siting to a gate which led down to a place Angels call the Abyss.

Ran looked over at Jude before he spoke, wishing for a moment of privacy. Jude did not seem to be paying any attention to them. He was using a rock to etch his name into the cave wall. Finally Ran leaned over and whispered to Katie, "I don't usually open up to people. But you are my friend, right?" Katie smiled at him, making him blush. "I've been really angry at God." Katie did not say anything. "I mean really, really angry. I was angry when my mom died. I was angry when we moved back to Indonesia. I was angry when I had to go to home school. I was especially angry because I missed my friends. And now I get back, expecting Gray to be my friend, and he's—well—you know."

"What?" Katie asked.

"He's different. I don't know if it's because of you or because of his parents' divorce. I just thought that when I got back, everything would work out a certain way, and it didn't. Did you know . . ." Ran was not sure if he should tell her. "Jude said he thinks Gray was responsible for making me fall."

Katie was shocked. "No way!"

"I don't know if I believe it or not, though."

As they were talking, little did they know, Jude was starting to feel very strange. For some unknown reason he was thinking the two were whispering about him and making fun of him. In fact, now that he thought about it, he was nothing but a third wheel. He watched as Katie opened her hand and placed it near Ran's. Then started wondering why he ever started hanging out with the dude that made Katie break up with Gray, his BEST friend. Then he began to wonder why he was hanging out with Katie, the girl who betrayed his best friend.

On the other side of the cave Ran and Katie stared at each other. Ran wanted to hold her hand, but was not sure if he should. He opened his hand. It was sweaty. He wiped it on his pants. Finally he decided not to. After all, he was not interested in girls. He was interested in football, music and school. Well, of course he was interested, but. . . well. . .

Jude clenched his fists. "You two can stay here and play kissy face, for all I care. I am going to go and find a way back home. This is crazy." He stomped out.

Ran and Katie looked confusingly at each other, then jumped up and chased after him, yelling, "Jude, come back here. We can't go out there. It's too dangerous."

Ran looked at Katie. "What's up with him?"

"I don't know, but we'd better go catch him before he leaves the cave." It was too late. Jude was already outside, making his way down the jagged rocks.

Katie looked at Ran. "What are we going to do?"

Ran sighed and grabbed Katie's hand. "We have no choice. We have to go get him." They started down the stony path after Jude. By the time they reached the bottom of the mountain, Jude was out of sight. The sun had set, though the moon was extraordinarily bright. They stared into the twilight, trying to see in which direction he had wandered off.

Katie opened her mouth to call out. Ran placed his hand over her lips and whispered, "We can't call out his name. It's too dangerous. We must remain very quiet." Behind them something stirred.

Katie grabbed Ran, "What was that?"

From behind the brush Clydesdale appeared. He was indignant. "What are you doing outside?"

Ran gulped, "Jude left the cave. We were trying to—"

Suddenly the ground shook. Clydesdale reared up on two legs. "Quick, get on my back—danger is near."

Ran could see that Katie was frightened as they mounted. "What is happening?" she asked in a not-so-brave tone, and she held tight to Ran.

"The T-Rex is approaching." Clydesdale did not hesitate. He was off in a dash. Looking over his back, he yelled, "Hold on tight."

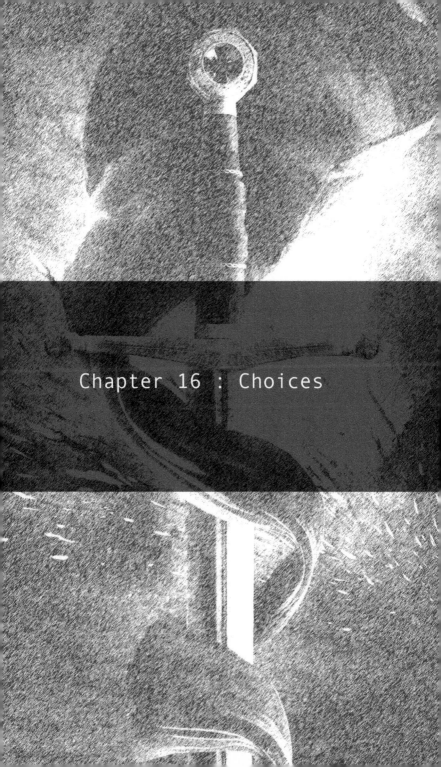

Chapter 16 : Choices

Choices

Eve, looking for dinner, walked through the Garden, unaware of any other event taking place. The Garden produced an array of choices. Her favorite part of searching for food was trying to find something she'd never eaten, and as she looked, she sang:

Beautiful garden,
Beautiful night,
Looking for berries
In the moonlight.
Maybe I'll find something
New to eat—
I hope that it's tasty,
I hope that it's sweet.

A voice from behind her spoke, "What a beautiful voice you have."

"Who is that?" Eve asked.

Snake appeared from behind a tree. "Don't be alarmed, my Queen, it isss only me."

"Oh, hello, Snake. What are you doing out of your den so late in the evening?"

"I couldn't sssleep, ssso I thought I would go out for a walk," Snake said. "With all due ressspect, my lady, what are you doing out?"

Eve walked toward Snake. She loved how reverent he was to her. Many animals in the garden had a hard time accepting her. Adam told her it was her imagination, but she could tell that some held no respect for her at all, except Snake. He always talked to her as if she was equal to Adam, and she was. She leaned against the tree. "I am out searching for dinner. Adam had something important to do with Lion."

Snake cringed at the mention of the name Lion. "Hmm, ssso what isss it you want to eat? I will go fetch it for you, my lady." He bowed his head.

"That's just the problem, Snake. I have tried most everything in the Garden and grow bored. There must be something I have not yet tasted."

Snake smiled. "Oh, but there isss, my Queen—over there." He pointed west. "There isss a tree."

Eve looked and recognized which tree he pointed toward. "Oh, no, dear Snake, we are not allowed to eat of the Tree of Knowledge of Good and Evil. Our Lord, God Almighty, forbids us."

"Yesss, ssso I heard." Snake slithered down to all fours and curled himself at her side. "I wonder why that isss?"

Eve looked down at him. "What do you mean?"

He slithered back up to stand near her ear. He whispered, "Do not tell anyone I told you, but every animal knowsss that your Lord only told you not to eat of the tree, becaussse he knowsss what will happen if you do."

"What will happen?"

"Hmm, I ssshouldn't tell you." He pulled back her hair as he whispered, "You will be like Him. You will be a god. He doesss not want that, doesss he?"

"I had no idea." Eve grabbed Snake by the hand. "Let's go over to the tree. I have never really looked at it."

"Yesss, my Queen. Pleassse lead the way."

Several miles east, Adam and Lion reached the cave to find it empty. Adam looked down at Lion. "I thought you said they stayed here for the night."

"They were supposed to, my lord." Lion looked at the cave wall. A name was etched in the stone. "Look here. One of their names has been carved in the rock. That means they were here."

"I wonder where they went?" Adam asked.

"I told you they were supposed to be leaving soon. They are probably long gone by now." Lion was relieved at the thought.

Adam and Lion walked out of the cave. "I am very hungry," Adam said. "I am going back to Eve now. She was supposed to find us something to eat." Adam raised his hand to his mouth and gave out a loud whoop.

Lion was curious. "What are you calling out for, sir?"

Before Adam could answer, Appaloosa galloped down the mountain and stood beside Adam.

Lion bowed his head. Adam mounted the horse, and off they trotted in the pale moonlight. As they were leaving, Adam turned back to Lion. "Watch the forest, my friend. I fear the night is still young and danger's still present." With these words he vanished into the night.

Lion decided he had better find out if the three humans were really gone. "I should have asked Appaloosa. Maybe Clydesdale or Stallion is near. I wish I could do that call my master does."

"Ouch!"

"Shhh!"

"I can't help it. I'm lying on something sharp. There, it

was a rock."

"Shut up!" Katie whispered to Ran. They were lying in tall brush with Clydesdale. So far, the T-Rex had not found them.

"No more talking, you two, I think he is near. If he is, he can probably smell us."

"How can we cover our smell?" Ran asked.

"I said be—" A noise interrupted Clydesdale. It was the snapping of a branch.

Katie turned around, "Behind you, Ran!"

From behind Ran the noise came. Through the brush Ran could see something in the darkness. He gulped. The bushes began to part. Something was coming near him. Clydesdale jumped up.

The figure yelled at them, "Ugh, you scared me."

It was Jude Tripp, "Guys, I'm sorry. I don't know what happened to me, I was sitting there when all the sudden. . ."

Clydesdale was impatient, "Get down, you imbecile, and be quiet. T-Rex is near."

It was too late. Just then the ground rumbled, and only yards away it roared, but not the kind of roar from a Hollywood movie. The sound was like the most evil growl from the pits of an evil abode.

"On my back, all three of you. Now!" Clydesdale commanded.

They mounted quickly and off he sprinted. Katie looked back over her shoulder. T-Rex was so close to them she could feel his hot breath on her neck. "Faster, Clydesdale, faster."

He ran through the woods with great speed, weaving through tree and brush. The dinosaur followed close after. His strides were too large.

The trail forked and Clydesdale chose right. He would

Chapter 16 : Choices

regret the choice later. They trotted down the mountain. On their left was the river, and on their right was an open pasture. To go left meant to drown, and to go right meant to risk running in the open field. Clydesdale had no choice.

The field was three hundred yards long and wide. At the end of the field was the tangled forest. It was the edge of the Garden, where no animal crossed.

If he could make it to the tangled forest, they would all be safe. He took a deep breath and sprinted into the open field. It was a trap. From every angle, animals came out of the tangled forest. They were soon surrounded. Above them Pterodactyl flew in circles, squealing with joy. Behind them was T-Rex. To the right was Komodo Dragon and Alligator. To the left were Stegosaurus and at least thirty lizards of all shapes, colors and sizes.

Alligator traipsed through the grass. "I told you I would be back to get you. What are you going to do now?"

Ran looked from one side to the other. He raised his fist. "By the authority of Adam, I command you to leave us alone."

The animals did not move. T-Rex began to laugh in a deep roar. The other animals surrounding them broke out into hysterical laughing.

Alligator chuckled, "We no longer answer to that name."

Just then, from behind them, a creature they had never seen joined the pack and stood beside Alligator. It was Snake.

He hissed, "Well done, my friends. Now let'sss rid thisss Garden of these unncccessssary fools.

Alligator was excited, "Did you do it?"

"Oh, and all too easy, my friend. Soon Adam will eat of it, too, and I will be your new king." Snake smiled and hissed, "What are we waiting for? Get rid of them." He pointed his finger at Ran, Katie and Jude.

"ROARRR! NOT SO FAST!" Lion stood behind them on the river's edge. I am still king of this Garden. Let them go—NOW!"

The animals did not move. "Have it your way." With these words, Lion began to roar louder than ever before. Then, from up the mountain, they began to come, every animal in the forest. First, was Bear, then Tiger and all cat like animals. The numbers they came in were so great that the valley was soon full and one by one they surrounded T-Rex, Komodo, Alligator, Stegosaurus and the lizards. Above them, large eagles and vultures surrounded Pterodactyl.

Lion spoke with authority, "Clydesdale, take them away now. Clydesdale began to back away toward the river's edge. He turned to go back up the mountain.

KABOOM! KABOOM!

Lightning flashed in the sky. Clydesdale reared up on two legs, frightened by a sound he had never heard. When he did, Katie lost her grip and fell into the river below.

Ran looked back. "Katie, hang on." But it was too late. She was swept by the current downriver. Ran did not hesitate. He jumped off the horse and plunged into the water.

"Wait. I will help you." Jude jumped in as well. The three were caught up in the current.

Clydesdale galloped alongside of them. "Can you find something to grab onto?"

But they could not. Only seconds later, they were out of sight.

Thunder rolled loudly through the sky, and wind whipped through the air. All of the animals scurried in fear. In the commotion, T-Rex, Komodo and Stegosaurus slipped away.

Lion saw Alligator and Snake trying to escape. "Stop right there, you two."

They turned around slowly. Snake spoke with a sly grin, "Sssomething ssstrange is happening. You are the king, Lion. You'd better find out what'sss going on before we all die."

Alligator laughed.

"Something strange, indeed," said Lion. He watched as the animals hid for cover. He did not know what to do. He stood there alone, his mane blowing in the wind.

Down the river Katie, Ran and Jude tried desperately to swim to the edge. Their efforts were futile. The wind made the water become rough. Some relief was found in the shape of a floating limb. Ran grabbed onto it first, and, one by one, Katie and Jude grabbed hold.

Ran held tight to Katie. "Just keep your head above water."

Jude's eyes grew wide. "That's going to be hard to do."

A hundred yards ahead was a waterfall. Katie cried, "We're going to die."

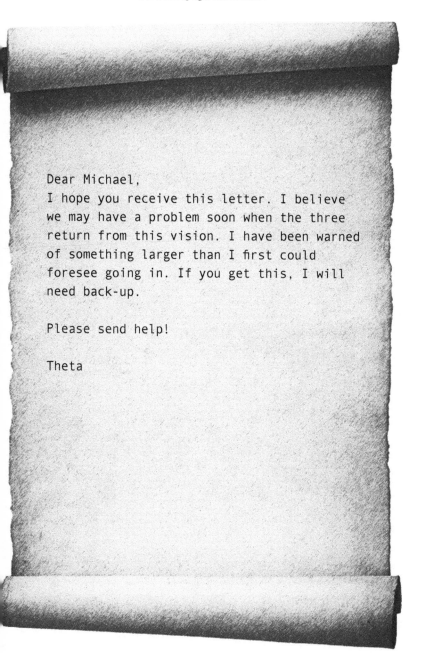

Dear Michael,
I hope you receive this letter. I believe
we may have a problem soon when the three
return from this vision. I have been warned
of something larger than I first could
foresee going in. If you get this, I will
need back-up.

Please send help!

Theta

Chapter 17 : Oops!

Oops!

Gray cupped his hands against the glass and stared into the professor's office window. "You think they'll be back soon?"

Vance was restless. "Come on, Gray, this isn't funny. The professor will kill us if he comes back."

"Be quiet, you coward. I'm going in." Gray walked around to the front door.

Vance quickly followed on his heels. "No, Gray! If you go in there, I'm leaving."

"What do you know, the door is open." Gray walked inside, and Vance followed reluctantly.

"What are you going to do?"

"You'll see," Gray said as he sneaked into Ran's room. The computer was on and glowing with swirling colors.

"Cool screensaver," Vance remarked.

"Yep, wait till he sees what I'm going to do to his computer," Gray laughed.

"What are you . . ."

Just then Gray did something that would have been cruel but wound up being to his misfortune: He punched the computer screen. But instead of his hand cracking the screen, as he desired, it vanished into the screen. And like those before him, his body followed.

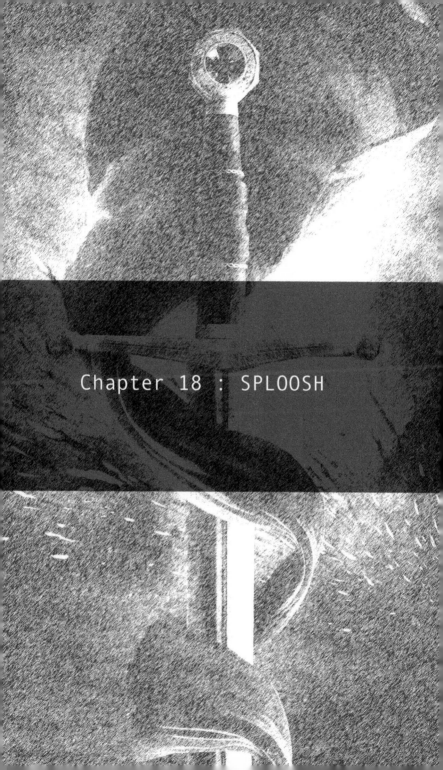

Chapter 18 : SPLOOSH

SPLOOSH

The edge of the waterfall was lined with gray, jagged rocks. Ran caught hold of one and Katie's hand at the same time. They dangled over the cliff, drenched and gasping for air.

Jude was not as lucky. Ran and Katie watched as his body plummeted, his arms flailing and his scream lost to the sound of the water's roar.

Then suddenly Ran and Katie watched a second body fall.

"Who was that?" Katie asked, and then she knew, "Gray!"

Ran's arms shook with exhaustion. "I can't hang on, Katie." The water rushed too quickly.

SPLOOSH!

They landed in the water below, each one struggling to the top and gasping for air.

Ran looked around quickly. "Is everyone all right?"

Katie and Jude answered, "Yes."

The three swam to shore and caught their breath. Drenched, they stood to their feet. Thunder rolled through the sky again. Looking on the other side of the sandy shore they saw Gray, bewildered and covered in seaweed.

"What's happening?" Gray asked as he looked up into the morning sky. "Where are we?"

"It's a little hard to explain."

Just then a body dropped into the water with a sploosh.

"Who is that?" Jude croaked.

Vance swam up and gasped for air. "Gray! What did you do to . . . Ran? Katie? Jude? What is going on?"

A voice spoke from a distance. It was a voice of authority. It was the Great Almighty God. "Adam and Eve, where are you hiding?"

In the distant valley, Ran saw two human figures creeping out of the bushes. They were clothed in leaves, but only the outline of their bodies looked human. They were beings of light.

He motioned to the gang to look.

Adam spoke first, "My Lord, we were ashamed, because we are naked."

"Who told you that you were naked?" the Lord asked. "Did you eat of the Tree of Knowledge of Good and Evil?"

The Almighty descended from the sky. He stood before Adam and Eve.

Ran, Katie and Jude covered their eyes, because the glory of the Lord shone brightly.

Jude whispered, "What's going on?"

"Shh. Just wait." Ran said.

Adam answered his Lord. "Sir, it was the woman you gave me. She gave me the fruit to eat."

The Lord looked at Eve. "What is this that you have done?"

Eve answered, "The Snake tricked me and I did eat."

Thunder rolled again and lightning struck near them. Frightened, Katie jumped up. "Let's get out of here."

Ran grabbed her arm. "Wait. Let's watch." They looked down in the valley.

Almighty God spoke again, "Where is Snake?"

Just then Aalok came out from behind the brush. "Here, my Massster."

Almighty God looked accusingly down on Snake. "Because you have done this, you are forever cursed above all cattle and above every beast of the field; upon your belly you will go, and dust will you eat all the days of your life. And I put enmity between you and the woman and between your seed and her seed: he shall bruise your head and you shall bruise his heel."

Then he looked at Eve with sorrow in his eyes. "Unto you,

Eve, I will greatly multiply your sorrow in your conception; in sorrow you will bring forth children; and your desire will be to your husband, and he will rule over you."

Turning to Adam he spoke again with great sorrow, "Unto you, Adam, because you listened to your wife and ate of the tree of which I commanded you, saying, 'You shall not eat of it,' cursed is the ground for your sake; in sorrow you will eat of it all the days of your life. Thorns and thistles it will bring forth to you, and you will eat the herb of the field. In the sweat of your face, you will eat bread until you return to the ground; for out of it I created you; for unto dust you are and unto dust you will return."

Adam began to weep desperately. He fell to his knees and put his hand to his face. Eve came behind him and held his shoulders as he shook with grief. She, too, cried for the grave mistake she had made.

The Almighty God commanded, "I will now clothe you."

Ran expected God to kill a sheep or something. Instead he watched as the light that once covered Adam and Eve faded and suddenly they were covered in skin, normal human skin. Ran then understood that there was probably a lot of other scriptures he thought he knew, but really didn't quite know.

From the heavens, a voice could be heard. It said, "Behold, the man is become as one of us, to know good and evil: and now, if he takes of the Tree of Life, and eats, he will live forever: Therefore, I must send him from the Garden in Eden."

Ran then also understood what the Garden really was.

Suddenly, from the sky, a great angel came down with a sword of fire, speaking with authority. "Leave this place immediately!"

Jude stood up and croaked, "Let's get out of here." With these words, Jude suddenly disappeared into a swirl of colors.

Katie looked at Ran. "What happened to—" She was next to disappear.

Gray seized Ran's arm. "You better tell me what's going ooooooooooooooon . . ." He was gone.

All Ran had to do was look at Vance to see he was afraid. His knees shook and his face was pale. Ran reached over and grabbed Vance by the hand. I'll explain everything when we get back." Vance disappeared.

Ran was alone in the Garden. He took one last look at Adam and Eve as they walked out of the Garden. He heard a sound and looked around. It was Lion. He looked very sad.

"I guess it is time for you to leave, my friend." Lion said.

"Yes. If I ever come back, will I see you?"

"I do not know. Promise me you will try."

Ran reached forward to touch Lion, but just then he felt his feet leave the ground. Colors swirled around him as he flew through the air.

The next thing he knew, he was standing in his bedroom. Katie and Jude were sitting on the bed.

"Wow, we're finally back." Jude, Katie and Ran all hugged. Ran sighed with relief to be home. "Hey, where's Gray and Vance?"

"They took out of here running. They are really scared," Jude laughed. "I think Gray peed his pants."

"That's not funny, Jude," Katie slapped his arm. "How did they find us?"

Ran said slowly, for he was exhausted, "I don't know. Look, we'd better find our folks and tell them what happened."

"Not so fast," a voice stopped him.

Ran glanced back at the computer. "Theta!" he exclaimed.

I surprised them by flying out of the screen, landing in the center of Ran's bedroom, my head almost touching the ceiling. "You did not miss any time at home. It is exactly four hours since you started studying."

"You mean no one knows we were gone?" Ran was amazed. All the time he had spent worrying was wasted.

"Before everyone goes their separate ways, I have a few questions. Who is the God of the Bible? Who is Man? Was there a Garden of Eden or a Garden IN Eden? Why did Adam and Eve choose their will over God's will? Lastly, where is the Garden now?"

"Katie, why don't you go first?" I recommended.

Katie stared at Ran, and Ran waited for her to answer. she said nervously. "The God of the Bible is more than some distant God. What I just saw made me realize, God is the father to all mankind."

That made me smile. "Who is Man then?"

Katie straightened up and answered confidently, "We

are God's children."

"Ran," I looked down into his eyes, "Tell me about the Garden IN Eden."

Ran smiled, "I learned something I never understood. The Garden was where Heaven met Earth. Adam and Eve lived between two realities, so to speak."

I think Ran could tell I was getting excited because he continued, "I think they allowed themselves to believe they could be equal with God. They thought they could do it without Him."

"How does that relate to the world today?" I probed.

Ran fumbled for words, "Wow, that's a hard one. . . I don't know." he answered honestly.

"That's okay," I assured him. "How about you, Jude, what do you think?"

I could tell Ran was a little nervous for Jude. He knew Jude did not seem to know much about this stuff.

"Hello, Jude, where are you?" I asked, searching the room.

All of us looked around for Jude. He was lying on Ran's bed under the blanket. Ran shook him. He peeked over the covers, then croaked, "What? I'm trying to sleep here."

"Jude, get up!" Ran said forcefully.

Jude rubbed his face. "All right, all right. What is it?"

Ran rolled his eyes, "Jude, Theta wants to know what you learned from going to Eden."

"Oh. Well, let me see." Jude sat up on the bed, rubbing the sleep from his eyes. "I learned that Adam and Eve are a couple of crazy people who exchanged paradise for a fallen and cursed world. They were tricked by a snake, they excluded their own Creator, and basically said they could do it all on their own. They completely forgot that without God they wouldn't even exist. . . And that sounds pretty much like the modern philosophy of today's world to me. Today, people think they can do everything on their own. Like my dad. That's why he won't go to church. No offense, Ran, but my dad thinks that church people are weak. And, to answer Theta's question, I learned that my dad is wrong. We do need God."

Ran and Katie exchanged looks of surprise.

"Wow, Jude, that was excellent," I smiled. "I can see you will do well. . . One more question, where is the Garden now?"

Katie jumped in, "You know what. I've heard Pastor Preacher say it's in Jerusalem and I've heard others say it's in Egypt or Etheopia, but I think they are all wrong."

"So where is it," I asked in earnest hope.

"It's in our heart," she said touching her chest and closing her eyes.

Something caught my eye just then, I looked over my shoulder. Ran felt chills run down his spine. Something strange was happening.

I unsheathed a shining silver sword. "Wait, Ran. Get down, everyone! I was afraid this might happen, just not so soon," he said.

From out of the computer an image emerged that Ran, Katie and Jude will never forget. From the screen a creature appeared—part beast, part angelic being. He was taller than Theta by several feet. The dark fallen angel crouched in the center of Ran's bedroom, and from out of his black cloak, his sharp talons gouged the air between them.

Katie and Jude jumped onto the bed. Ran stood between the creature and Theta.

That's when something horrible happened, "Get out of the way!" I cried, but it was too late. The creature arose, reaching out his animal-like claw, clamped down, snatching

Ran up like a rag doll.

"Take your hands off of God's chosen!" I commanded, with my sword pointing at the demon. The sharp tip was an uncomfortable few inches away from Ran.

The creature merely laughed at me with sinister enjoyment, for the fallen are dark characters of old. This one was particularly disgusting. His cloak was ash gray, and his skin was mostly dark red and pink in splotches around his muzzled nose. Horns came not from his head, as many think, but like large tusks from his spit-drooling mouth.

"If you want the boy, end this mission," he hissed, and green goo oozed from his lips down his yellow tusks and onto Ran's shoulders.

"Who are you?" I probed.

"I am Leviathan, Prince of the Abyss and Master of the Realm of Time. These visions will end or I will release my armies against you!" His claws dug deep into Ran's throat.

Ran was not breathing.

"These visions will not stop, for they have been commanded by God Almighty. Now unloose the boy or meet the end of my sword."

The spirit spewed his hot breath over Ran. "I guess you forget: I don't take orders from angels."

"No, that's right. You and your kind just followed the darkest angel of them all—Lucifer."

"You will shut your mouth, Theta. I am taking the boy with me."

"No! He's not ready to battle you," I cried, raising my sword.

"You should have thought of that before you started this mission." Leviathan turned and dropped Ran on the floor. Pointing the palm of his slimy, paw-like hand at Ran, he seethed an ancient curse through his crooked brown teeth,

"Dies, diei, custodiae, custodie, leodie, malbodiensis."

Ran's legs felt cold, like he was in freezing water. His legs were frozen, and the words were like icicles spoken over him. His eyes blurred, shutting closed. He tried to open them and then lost balance. Groping blindly, he tripped and fell to his left. His arm caught the fall. His arm hurt, but it was nothing compared to what was going on inside his mind. He began to see flashes of his father—short flashes. Some were memories and some were not. The ones that were not memories were like still shots or short films inside his mind. He watched as his father was hit over the head by the terrorist in Indonesia.

He screamed, "NO, STOP! DON'T HURT HIM."

Katie and Jude held each other in the corner of Ran's room. Leviathan was repeating the ancient curse over again.

I wasted no time. I plunged toward Leviathan, with the tip of my sword pointed toward him.

Leviathan stopped speaking the curse and turned away to defend himself. Moving to one side, he barely escaped my blade, then he unsheathed his sword and took his stance.

The fight was on!

I had never faced a man or beast of Satan with as much power and skill as this horrid creature. He was too much for me. I was no match. My sword was quickly flung out of my reach, giving the beast a moment to turn back on Ran.

He spoke again in an ancient language only I understood: "Lacrima heliandum!"

Katie grabbed tighter at Jude's arm, yelling, "What is he saying?"

I said, "He just called for help."

From out of the computer screen, four creatures just

as nasty as the first appeared, flooding the room with the stench of death. Four swords drawn, eyes piercing green, the demons mockingly smiled at me.

There was nothing I could do. I was cornered. I gripped my sword tightly, but at once they were upon me with sounds of clanging swords, shouts and seething laughter, their strength beyond mine.

Ran wanted to help, but it was too late for me. I was overtaken.

The four demons bound and beat me, and as quickly as they had appeared, they were gone through the computer screen, taking me with them.

Back in Ran's room, Leviathan, perching like a toad, again stretched out the palm of his hand toward Ran and resumed speaking his ancient curse. Ran's eyes shut tight again. The images came faster and stronger. He tried to think of something—anything else. He heard Jude saying something, but could not make it out.

Jude had been watching the entire tragedy unravel when a thought came to him. He remembered back—back when Ran was surrounded by reptiles. He recalled how Ran had spoken in the authority of the name of Adam and the reptiles had to leave. He remembered Ran telling him that demons are the same, except Ran said that a Christian had to use the authority of the name of Jesus.

Jude screamed at the top of his voice to get Ran's attention: "Ran, use the name of Jesus!"

Ran heard Jude scream again, but what was he saying? Ran tried to listen, but just then the images came too strong to resist. Ran watched his father enter the church building the day of his murder. He saw him put the key in the door, and he saw the terrorist on the other side, waiting. He watched as they beat him and tied him up. Then he watched as they set fire to the church. Then somehow, through the images, came the voices of Jude and Katie, screaming loudly:

"IN THE AUTHORITY OF JESUS CHRIST, GET OUT OF HERE, YOU CREATURE OF HELL! WE COMMAND YOU RIGHT NOW!"

Suddenly the weight of the room lifted, and light cut through the darkness of Ran's bedroom.

Leviathan, was gone.

Katie leapt from the corner and threw herself down on the floor beside Ran. "Are you all right?"

Ran rubbed his eyes. "Yes . . . I think so. What happened?"

Jude put out his hand and helped Ran up to sit on his bed. "You were under attack," Jude said. "We just did what you taught us."

"What I taught you?" Ran was amazed. He never thought he could be a teacher of something so awesome.

The door opened. "Hello, my little sweeties," Grandma Wisdom said, as she cracked the door open and peeked in. "How is the studying going?"

Ran, Katie and Jude looked at each other and answered in unison, "Fine."

"I just got back from church. Be quiet when you leave, please. Grandpa is resting on the couch."

A car horn honked. "That must be Katie's mother," Grandma smiled. "Katie, it was nice having you. Come back soon to study."

Katie smiled at Granny Wisdom and said, "Thank you

for allowing me to come." She looked back at Ran, feeling awkward. "Um, I'll see you at school tomorrow. Take care."

Ran walked with her to the door. He whispered so as not to wake his grandfather, "Hey, I had a really great time. We need to, like, sit down and talk about all this."

The annoying croak of Jude's voice interrupted, "Hey, we've got to write a paper about this, and what about the next chapter? Are we going to have to go back into that computer . . ."

Ran put his hand over Jude's mouth, "Shh. Don't wake Grandpa." Then Ran whispered through his teeth, "Don't say a word about this to anyone. Do you hear me? They will think we're crazy."

"Sorry, dude," Jude croaked loudly.

Ran and Katie both said, "Shh . . ."

Ran opened the door, and the three went out on the front porch. The sun was shining brightly in the blue sky. "Crazy Arkansas weather," Ran mumbled.

Katie's mother was waiting in her SUV. She rolled down the window, "Let's go honey."

Katie looked at Ran, wishing for a moment alone to tell him what all was going through her mind. She wanted to tell him how happy she was that he had moved back and how much she enjoyed being in Eden with him. She wished she could open her heart and pour out the secrets, but instead she said, "I'll see ya, Ran."

With that, she turned and walked toward the SUV. Ran watched the vehicle drive away. He turned and saw Jude still standing there. "Hey, do you need a ride?"

"Huh?" Jude was looking up at the sky.

"I was wondering if you needed a ride or to use the phone."

"Oh, no, thanks, I'm walking over to Gray's house. He invited me to spend the night, and I was just waiting a second for Katie to leave. I was going to tell you something."

"Wait a second," Ran said. "You're going to spend the night with Gray—after what he did to me? What are you going to tell him about what's happened?"

"Did you see his face when he and Vance landed in Eden? I wonder how that happened."

Ran put his hand on his head. It was still aching. "I don't know, but maybe you can find something out when you're over there."

"This has been a crazy day," Jude said, as he stared out at the clouds still left from the storm. "Did we really do all of that?"

"I don't know. It was like a dream. What was it Theta said about it being like a vision?" Ran asked. "Hey, wait! Theta! He was taken by those creatures. I totally forgot when Granny came in the room."

Ran and Jude ripped open the screen door and sprinted to Ran's room. Ran grabbed the mouse on his computer. The screen went from black to white, and there I was, hovering in the center of the screen.

"Theta, are you okay?" Ran asked.

"Fit as a fiddle, thanks to the prayers of Jude and Katie. You three are going to make quite a dynamic team. I'll see you soon."

With these words I waved, turned, and flew into the white background of the screen and back to prepare for the next adventure.

"Wow," croaked Jude. "I can't wait until next time."

Ran smiled, "Yeah, next time."

If you read the first book you are now part of the story. Pray God reveals to you His destiny for you. If you desire to ask Jesus into the Garden of you heart, now is the time. He is a real living God who loves you and desires to let you know His love toward you.

To share His love with others, simply ask God if there is anyone with whom He is asking you to share this book.

You can help me by passing these documents on to others.

Others who are in your "Chosen Generation".

With Much Love and Until Next Time!

Theta

Epilogue

Mission 1   :   Eden

Status   :   Accomplished

Mission 2   :   Noah

Agenda   :   Continue discipleship
                with Ran, Katie and Jude

Specific Target : Jill Denver

*"And so the mystery begins.
Looking forward to the next book in the series."*

Ian Clayton
Son Of Thunder

Special Thanks

A special heartfelt thanks to all my family and friends who supported this endeavor, reading several unpolished versions and listening to plot ideas. You were always helpful with suggestions. Thank you to my two older brothers. There is not enough room here to say the words, but you know.

Next, Jan Sligh for editing the first version and Sister Katherine Whitney (my mentor, teacher, editor, and grandmother in the faith) for editing the final copies. Sister Whitney, my Granny Wisdom, you are now among the cloud of witnesses, and I have no doubt you are witnessing on my behalf. Also, I thank Author John L. Moore for reading the manuscript and giving me helpful advice.

Thank you to my father and mother, who pray daily for me and do not give up on me, even though I am your artistic and in times past a wayward son. You are the models I look to for an example of how Christ loves. I love you! I hope this book is a testimony of seeds you have sewn in me.

Most importantly, I thank my Heavenly Father. Once upon a time, I thought I chose Him. Thank you, God, for choosing me.

About the Author

Brad Parker lives with his wife and children in rural Arkansas where he writes fiction for all ages. His personal goal is to tell stories of hope for the future.

SeraphCreative

Heaven's Heart for Earth

Seraph Creative is a collective of artists, writers, theologians & illustrators who desire to see the body of Christ grow into full maturity, walking in their inheritance as Sons Of God on the Earth.

Sign up to our newsletter to know about the release of the next book in the *Chosen Generation* series, *Mission 2 : Noah*, as well as other exciting releases.

Visit our website :
www.seraphcreative.org

THE FELLOWSHIP
OF THE FLAME